ADVENTURES

into the

UNKNOWN

Russ Crossley

with

R.G. Hart

3RD STREET PUBLISHING

Dedication

For Mom and Dad. I miss you both, love you always.

Adventures into the Unknown

Logo image by:

Engraver | Dreamstime.com

Published by 53rd Street Publishing
www.53rdstreetpublising.com

Table of Contents

Introduction

One of the many things I love about fiction writing is the ability of the author to smash ideas together to come up with new original ideas. I particularly love to create odd characters and place them in unusual circumstances. This is what makes writing and reading fun and interesting for me, and hopefully you as well.

In this collection you will find spies, detectives, and heroes who aren't necessarily human. And you will find stories involving time travel, or of alternate realities, or strange realities where normal is often very different than the reality we live in.

The last story in the collection is by paranormal romance author, R.G. Hart. The story involves his on-going character, Aloha Armstrong (aka The Woman From L.I.P.S.). Aloha also appears in a new original novel entitled, Zomopolis. I encourage you to look for this thrilling romantic adventure of a very unique secret agent.

The ten tales in this collection will transport you to some wonderful places where you will find sadness, hope, sacrifice, and maybe even a smile or two.

I hope you enjoy them. If you wish to provide feedback please feel free to contact me on twitter or Facebook or via one of my websites.

Enjoy.

Russ Crossley
Vancouver B.C.
July 2013

Shoeless Moe

THE DAY SHE CALLED ME I sat at my cigarette scarred desk in the dimly lit newsroom with nothing to write about. The city editor had just killed my series about the mob's control of the unions. The editor said they were poorly written pieces. But I knew the real reason was he was getting pressure from the boy's downtown. The mob was throwing a lot of green around these days, and the politico types had become the mob's lap dogs.

She told me her name was Old Woman and that she lost a shoe, a really big shoe. Old Woman claimed she lived in the shoe with so many kids she didn't know what to do.

A fact that would lead to her death, and my arrest for her murder.

My name's Rumplestiltskin. I'm a reporter for Big City Bugle newspaper, and my beat is the night desk.

Like every dame in Big City I knew right away she was working an angle. Red headed dames are the trickiest ones. I called up her picture up on the worldwide web as we talked. I saw a woman with hair the color of carrots, so her intentions were immediately clear. And I'm a confirmed blonde man, but redheads and brunettes are okay by me.

1

Shoeless Moe

From the moment I heard her sweet talk a sour feeling grew deep in my gut. But my weakness for the fairer sex too often gets me in deep.

We agreed to meet on the wrong side of the tracks, out near the Moldy Projects, named after Rusk Moldy, the crooked developer. As it usually does in Big City it was raining hard by the time I got there.

I had the collar of my trench coat pulled up tight around my pointed ears, and shivered when a cold raindrop fell off the brim of my grey felt fedora to run down my neck. That was when I spotted her standing in the yellow light of a street lamp smoking a long cigarette. I licked my lips, and for the millionth time this week, suppressed the urge to bum a smoke. I always pick the lousiest times to give up a perfectly good vice.

Tall and willowy, her makeup heavy, so thick in fact it looked like it had been applied with a pallet knife. Her full lips were painted red, and her pea green eye shadow emphasized her almond shaped eyes. As I got closer I realized she was much older than she looked from a distance. But then I'm a four hundred year old troll so who am I to call the witches cauldron black?

As I stepped from the thick shadows into the pale light of the street lamp her emerald eyes smiled at the same time as her sensual mouth. Good thing. If I had thought this was a trap I would have used the .38 I kept in the shoulder holster hidden beneath my gray trench coat. The one the cops don't know about.

I hadn't shaved in a coupla days, and my breath probably reeked of the shot of cheap whisky I drank before leaving the office, but hey in my line of work I'm what's referred to as the diamond-in-the-rough.

When Mrs. Woman telephoned she told me her giant shoe had disappeared. When I asked her what she meant by disappeared she explained she'd been on a date with a man and when she came back it wasn't where she left it.

Now in Big City a missing shoe isn't news, unless it's five stories high, and her date is with Milo Grimm, Capo for the Grimm Brothers mob. This dame had gotten my attention.

The Grimm's control the rackets on the west aide. Every speakeasy, gin joint, pimp, and gambling den pays the Grimm's protection money. Any who refuse disappear into Never Never Land. I've known a few city editors who I often wished would double cross the Grimm's so they'd disappear, but then who'd be stupid enough to cross the Grimm's?

My well-tuned reporter seventh sense told me the dame was gonna make one heck of a story, and I wanted in on the ground floor.

"Hey, doll," I kept my tone light. My let's-be-friends mode was set on charming.

She regarded me coolly as I watched rain drip off the edge of her wide brimmed hat. One perfectly plucked eyebrow arched on her pale forehead. Under her gaze I felt the familiar twinge in that nice-ta-meet-ya place.

"You Rumplestiltskin?" Naturally she already knew who I was, or she wouldn't have been standing under this street lamp. Playing dumb was a way of life in the underbelly of the Big City. Always force the other guy to show his hole card first. She is a clever gal this one.

"Yes, ma'am." I grinned.

Her eyes narrowed and she took a drag on her cigarette, held it for a second or two, then blew the smoke in my face. I blinked and coughed. "Want one?" Evidently she recognized a reformed nicotine addict when she saw one.

"No. Thanks." I wiped the tear from my left eye with the back of one hand.

Her voice was husky with an extra layer of sexy. "So, Mr. Rumplestiltskin, can you help me find my lost shoe?"

"Sure," I nodded, "I know a few people in this town. I'm pretty certain someone'll know who stole a size way-too-big-for-us-normals shoe." I shrugged. "I mean who wants a giant shoe?

Her pencil thin eyebrows shot up. "A woman with too many children, perhaps?" There was an amused edge in her tone.

I nodded and stuffed my hands in the pockets of my trench coat. "Yeah. I know a little about rug rats."

"Really? You don't look like the child-friendly type to me."

I grinned. "I wasn't always a Big City byline ya know." Her sensuous mouth broke into a pleasant smile then she laughed brightly.

How do ya like that? I made a funny, even though I didn't mean to be funny. Now boyo, I cautioned myself, don't let her flattery cause your head to swell to the size of your ego. You're not that funny. I looked around. "So where was this shoe when it went missing?"

She shook her head. "I said it disappeared, remember?"

"Yeah. Sorry. Is there a difference?"

She ignored my question. "Follow me." She wiggled an index finger to beckon me to walk with her out of the protection of the street lamp and into the inky darkness.

When I followed her into the blackness outside the circle of light of the street lamp it was as if I'd suddenly gone blind. I couldn't see even my hand, or anything else, in front of my face. The world disappeared in black ink. She instructed me to look straight ahead and avoid looking back at the light, so my eyes would adjust to the darkness. Old said she wanted me to see something. Something important.

As we stood side-by-side I heard her breathing and smelled her cheesecake-scented perfume. I've never enjoyed sweet desserts, even feminine ones. They rot your teeth and your mind at the same time, and usually they steal your wallet before you wake up in the morning.

After about five minutes of silence, the only sound the pounding of rain off the cracked and oily pavement; my eyesight had adjusted enough so I could make out two abandoned brick walkups. Between them was a large gap. Could this be where the giant shoe once stood?

If it was then this thing had left one colossal footprint. I would hate to meet the owner of a shoe that big. I frowned. If she lived in one giant sized shoe I wondered where the other half of the pair was.

My answer was a sharp blow to the back of the head and the world disappeared.

* * *

When I woke it was morning. I opened my eyes looking into a face only a bulldog would love. Lieutenant Manny "Mother" Goose of Big City PD's Homicide Division glowered at me from under the brim of his chocolate brown fedora. He gnawed at his unlit cigar that hung from the side of the slash in the middle of his jowly mug; I loosely refer to as a mouth. Mother and I gave up smoking on the same day. It wasn't a good day. I hoped today would be better, but somehow I doubted it.

"Rump, you alive?"

"Unless you're the devil welcoming me to hell, yeah I'm alive." My voice sounded like sandpaper. When his expression didn't change I added, "What happened?"

I groaned when I tried to raise my head and pain shot across my forehead and my guts twisted. I was going to vomit for sure. I eased my head back to the ground and closed my eyes and waited for the nausea to pass.

"Somebody knocked your noodle into next week," said Mother.

My eyes fluttered open and I blinked to clear the fog in my head. "Now I know why you're the detective and I'm the lowly reporter."

As my vision cleared I saw the sky above was gray with billowing, angry clouds, but at least it wasn't raining. Yet.

I managed to raise to myself to my elbows as Mother stepped back, his thumbs hooked off the pockets of the vest under his cheap wool suit jacket. He turned his back to me to face the abandoned buildings.

My eyes narrowed as I studied my surroundings. The two abandoned brick walkups were still there, rust-colored bricks covered with black mold. Between them was the largest footprint I'd ever seen. Old Woman clearly wasn't exaggerating. The shoe had to be at least a size four hundred, triple E.

"Where's the dame?" I asked.

Mother glanced over his shoulder at me and nodded to a spot beside me surrounded by banana-yellow caution tape. In the middle of the tape was a puddle of goo. "That's what's left," he said casually.

My eyes went wide and I froze. "What happened?"

"Somebody slimed her," he said simply.

"I can see that, Mother, but who and why?"

"We're not sure why yet, but we suspect it was a lovers spat, or maybe an attempted rape." He paused and swung round to face me.

"You and I've known each other a long time, eh Rump?"

I nodded slowly. I didn't like where he was going with this line of questioning. "Yeah. Sure, Mother you and I go way back. We had some good times and a few giggles."

Mother shrugged and sighed. "Yeah. Good times." His words trailed off. Suddenly his eyes locked on mine. "Listen, Rump I have my orders. People farther up the food chain smell blood. I'm sure you understand."

My mouth twisted in a sardonic grin. "I'm under arrest, right?"

Mother winced like he'd sucked on a lemon and nodded.

I sat up feeling suddenly better. My headache was nearly gone and the knot in my stomach had eased. It all made sense. A for-show arrest, then Mother would vouch for me, and I'd be back at my desk before noon writing the story of the missing giant shoe, the mobster romance gone sour, and the cheesecake scented puddle of goo. What a story this was gonna be.

"I know what you're thinkin', Rump but it's not gonna be that simple," Mother's mouth became a grim line.

I looked at him and frowned. "What do you mean? It's ridiculous to think I'd kill a dame I just met." I walked toward the gap where the giant shoe print was clearly visible in the light brown soil and waved my arm at it to emphasize my point. "I wouldn't kill a woman I hated, never mind some gal I just met. And I only met her because she called me and asked me to meet her here." I scowled at him. Now I was plain old mad. This was the biggest injustice since that idiot baked blackbirds in a pie.

"I think you better hold on, Rump and stop talking. I have to read you your rights so you shouldn't say nothin' without a legal eagle present."

I stared at Mother and realized he was serious. I felt my face grow flush with anger. "You can't be serious about charging me?"

Ignoring me, as if I were a common criminal, Mother pulled back one side of my suit jacket and pulled my .38 from my shoulder holster as he began to recite my rights. "Rumplestiltskin, you have the right…"

I didn't listen to the rest. I knew it by heart anyway. Working the night beat you see a lot of arrests. I could never figure out why criminals always seem to work at night. Especially murderers. What's wrong with murdering someone in the afternoon, or before lunch? At least then you'd have the rest of the day to do what you want.

But nope, not in Big City. In Big City murders happen after sunset.

I glanced at the goo. She may have been old, but she was a looker. Mother was right about two things; I just met the Old Woman who lived in a shoe, and I was gonna miss her.

I narrowed my eyes to slits. There was something very wrong with all this.

"Do you understand these rights as I have explained them?" finished Mother in the familiar bland monotone he used for all his arrests.

"Yeah, sure. Whatever. But, Mother explain this to me, how do you know this goo is her goo?" I indicated the gelatinous substance behind the yellow tape with a slight nod of my head. I sniffed the air. "And I smell Cinnamon not cheesecake." I felt a growing sense of excitement. I was onto something and my reporter instincts were in high gear.

Mother looked at me as if I'd grown two heads. The cheesecake part is probably a little over the top.

"The lab boys ran some tests," Mother shrugged his wide shoulders. He pulled his handcuffs from the leather holder on his belt and came toward me. "Put both hands on your head, then place one hand behind your back."

When Mother came up behind me to snap the handcuffs round my wrists I smelled his warm garlic breath then I heard him whisper, "Run."

I had a split second to decide if I should. Naturally, I always follow whispered instructions so I elbowed Mother in the gut. He grunted and I took off running across the gap between the buildings.

I've never been a runner so before I went fifty feet I was breathing hard and sweat poured down my leathery face. My mouth felt like it was crammed full of cotton balls.

I heard a voice behind me that wasn't Mother's yell for me to stop or he'd shoot. I didn't stop and I didn't look back. What I did do was will my rubbery legs to carry me faster and faster.

The distinct sound of a pistol hammer being cocked echoed off the buildings on either side of me. I knew I was seconds away from death by .38 police special. I kept my feet moving. But it was like I was running underwater, because I seemed to be going slower and slower.

I almost made it to the far edge of the buildings, where I'd be able to take cover, when a shot rang out. I tripped and fell face first hard into the mud.

I thought at first I was hit, but there wasn't any pain so I knew he'd missed.

"Rump! Move your butt!" I raised my head and wiped away the mud from my eyes. When I was able to see again I looked back and saw Mother had his gun out and was urging me on with it. I froze when I saw the trial of smoke coming from the barrel and the unmoving uniformed cop lying face down in front of him.

I realized Mother had set me up as a cop killer. Now every cop in Big City would be gunning for me. I wasn't wanted dead or alive, I was wanted sooo dead. Et tu, Mother?

* * *

Someone had bought off the locals to make sure I was edited out of the picture. But why kill the girl? And why steal a big shoe? This wasn't making a lot of sense.

I ran up the steps of the brownstone tenement building of the Van Allen Belt working class neighborhood taking two stairs at a time. I was breathing hard as I stood outside apartment 4C.

Along the way here I had stopped in City Park to wash the mud off as best I could in the public restroom. Three junkies slept peacefully in the stalls when I was running water in the sink. The towel dispenser had stood empty for over twenty years so I was forced to cup water in my palms and scoop it to wash the mud off my clothes and face. The water reeked of rust and decay. Like everything else in this rot infested town the water had even turned on me.

My only hope now was to get out of Big City. And my secretary Cindy Charming was the only hole card left to play. After all she owed me.

I helped her escape the Prince's castle in the bad old days, when the heavy drinking prince had threatened to murder her, and brought her to Big City.

I rapped on the door. The sound echoed down the long hallway. In less than a minute the door opened a crack. The steel chain was visible across the opening. One inquisitive azure eye peered at me.

"Mr. Rumplestiltskin is that you?" Cindy stepped back and the chain rattled against the doorframe then the door swung open. Cindy wore a slip-over-your-head, floor-length powder blue housecoat that accented her honey blonde hair. The housecoat was closed up to her slender neck.

I never had romantic designs on Cindy. She was young when I brought her here and I considered her my little sister. When we first arrived in Big City I worried her innocence might be corrupted by the dirt and squalor all around us. But she remained the one good person I knew in this town.

I walked in the apartment and closed the door behind me with a thump.

Cindy's apartment matched her personality. A pink throw rug sat under a pine coffee table in front of a pure white sofa. Mustard yellow curtains framed the windows overlooking the street below. A dozen red roses rested in a crystal vase on an end table to the left of the sofa. Their fragrance filled the room.

I looked down at my clothes and hands and realized I better stay right here by the door. There was no way I was going to track mud on her perfect domestic tranquility.

"Mr. Rumplestiltskin what's happened to you?" Cindy left the room momentarily and came back with a towel.

I thanked her and began to dry my face, hands and hair. "We have to get out of town." Her eyes were wide. "Today, Cindy. We have to leave."

She looked at me dumbfounded as if I were speaking a foreign language. "Cindy, if we don't leave today I will die. Do you understand?"

She nodded and her brow furrowed. "Yes, I do but I'm not leaving."

My jaw dropped and I gapped at her. "What are you talking about? Didn't you hear what I said?"

Cindy nodded grimly. "Yes, as I said already I understand but you're on your own. I'm staying." The determination in her tone made me wonder what happened to Cindy Charming, my little sister, and who was this woman standing before me.

"Cindy, what's the matter with you?"

"Nothing. I have a benefactor. He takes care of me."

A benefactor? My gut twisted. Someone had taken advantage of this sweet young girl and corrupted her. 'Who is it?" I asked between gritted teeth.

"Milo Grimm," she said confidently. She crossed her arms over her chest and turned her back on me.

"He told me he was going to set you up for a murder rap because he was hurt by the lies you wrote in the newspaper about his business."

I couldn't believe what I was hearing. "But, Cindy Milo Grimm is a mobster, a criminal. He's using you."

She sniffed. "He said you'd say that." Cindy whirled to face me; her normally gentle features were marred by a scowl. "Just because someone's in the bar business everyone assumes they're mobbed up.

"Milo thought about paying you off, but I told him not to. I know you too well. You're a troll with principals." She scoffed. "Principals that'll land you in the gas chamber."

I let out an exasperated grunt like I'd just been punched in the gut. "Cindy, I thought we loved each other."

Someone pounded on the door interrupting us. We looked at each other. "Are you expecting someone else?" She shook her head.

"See who it is and I'll hide in the bathroom." I hurried to the bathroom and closed the door behind me. I climbed into the bathtub and pulled the shower curtain across. Unlike my bathroom that hadn't been cleaned in five months hers smelled of lavender and Ivory soap.

I listened intently. I heard her soft tone speaking, not the exact words just a murmur. Then suddenly there were angry words and the thump, thump of pounding feet then the bathroom flew open and thudded against the wall cracking the plaster.

"Rump? It's Mother. You can come out now. It's all over."

I slid the shower curtain aside and saw Mother in his protective vest with his gun in his right hand. He wore a silly grin on his face.

"Did you get him?"

"Yeah," Mother nodded. "Found Milo hiding in a secret passageway in the lady's bedroom." He stuffed his gun back in his shoulder holster then accompanied me to the living room.

Upon entering the room I discovered Cindy and Milo seated side by side on the sofa glaring at the two uniforms standing over them. They weren't going to say anything more, at least not until they met with their lawyer, and probably not even then. We had plenty of Cindy on tape to convict them both for racketeering and conspiracy. It was enough to send them both up the river for long stretches.

I frowned. "Something I don't get, Mother. How do Old Woman and the disappearing giant shoe fit into this?"

Mother laughed. "They don't. We found Old Woman's husband. The shoe is his. When he left town some year's back, he left one shoe behind for good luck. Old woman who has so many children knew exactly what to do, she moved her kids into it."

"So who's her husband?"

Mother grinned. "He plays baseball for the Neverland Giants. They call him Shoeless Moe. His real name is Moe Fofum."

I shook my head and chuckled. "I get it. Moe's a giant."

Mother nodded. "Yup, 'bout as big as they get. His nickname's shoeless because he only wears one shoe when he plays. He came home to retrieve the other one. He told me the kids moved out of the shoe years ago, but his wife loved living in it. A lot more room in a giant shoe that a one bedroom apartment these days."

"You spoke to him?"

Mother nodded. "Yeah. Heck of a nice guy for a giant."

"And I assume Old Woman's not dead," I paused, "but what about the goo?"

He shook his head. "Hair gel. Moe wears the stuff his sponsor gives him. Practically bathes in it."

I chuckled and nodded then glanced at Cindy. She avoided looking at me.

I may never write the story about all this. There is just so much pain and heartbreak one reporter can take after another day on the night beat —

— the night beat in Big City.

Hero for A Day

It's good to be Mother Nature.

Especially when you're the guest of honor at the Mythic Alliance of Creatures (the MAC for short) annual convention in Mythopolis City.

It was the first day of the convention when I first laid eyes on Kris. He stood beside the entrance to the exhibit hall in front of the registration table. Jack Frost and Cupid were handing him his nametag as I walked up beside him.

Jack grimaced when he spotted me. The icy little creep's face was blue as the Antarctic sea with horror. He had suffered my wrath more than once over eternity. He didn't care for my style.

Since I planned to give away a Get-Out-of-Wrath free card at the charity auction later in the conference he might yet win my reprieve. But I doubted it. His luck had always been cold.

I don't much care for the cold. Makes growing trees, flowers, and grass more of a challenge.

Let me tell you about Kris. He was one handsome Mythic in those days. A long white beard, curly hair the color of new snow, a dashing fire engine red two-piece suit, and matching shoes made him the bell of the ball to my eyes.

"Hi," he said his cheery red lips and rosy cheeks glowing as he turned to grin at me. "I'm Kris Kr—"

"Nice to meet you," I interrupted him. "First time?" What was I thinking? I was acting like a schoolgirl.

When he smiled his blue eyes, the color of a summer day, sparkled. And I don't mean I imagined it like in the romance novels. They actually sparkled!

(Yes, Mother Nature reads romance novels. I can't be all business all the time ya know.)

"Yes, actually I—" Kris said.

"Oh, you'll love it," I said. I wanted to die and drop into a hole. Do I ever shut up?

Cupid flapped his wings and flew between us. "Uhhh…do have your registration receipt there, Toots?"

I glared at the little winged puke. He wasn't Mr. Tact at the best of times. And he reeked of chocolate. How could anyone eat something manufactured from a bean as bitter as cocoa?

I only eat raw foods. One hundred percent natural and organic is the only way to go. At least that's what I'm told.

The nerve. Imagine calling me Toots! Cupid was lucky Kris was there or I would have blown him to Timbuktu.

"You flying rodent I was talking to the convention rooki—" I looked around Cupid in time to see Kris stroll through the doors and disappear into the exhibit hall.

"Well. There's no need to be rude," Cupid sniffed.

I reached into the pocket of my skirt to pull out my receipt. I stepped around Cupid, who still hovered in front of me, and dropped my receipt on the table. Without hesitation Jack picked it up and handed me my pre-made nametag. He wanted me gone.

I started for the doors in the hope I would find Kris. I felt a breeze and detected the scent of cocoa coming up fast from astern. I stopped short and felt Cupid bounce off the back of my head.

Good thing he's lighter than air or he could have really hurt himself.

Without looking back I said, "It's not good to fool with Mother Nature." I heard a satisfying flutter of tiny wings move away followed by the sound of ice cracking under pressure.

My stride increased. That'll show 'em.

Once inside the massive convention hall I saw a maze of display booths. The Easter Bunny had his egglets on display, as he did every year. Father Time was selling the perpetual calendars again this year. Why? I have no idea. Once you had one of his calendars you never need another.

I hurried passed the Tooth Fairy's booth and saw she had something new this year. A baby teeth display complete with x-rays. Cool.

I finally spotted Kris ahead of me standing in front of the Fairy Godmother's booth. He was staring into an empty glass case. Odd.

I had been running full steam so I pulled up and slowed to what I hoped looked like a casual stroll.

I could see my lonely-hearts ad now: Long strolls on the beach, candle light dinners, opera, theatre, and time travel. Lonely Mythic seeks heroic companion to spend eternity with. I sighed at the thought.

Yes, I admit it I'm lonely. You try being responsible for an entire eco-system, tornadoes, floods, hurricanes, everything and still find time to meet that someone special. Get real, people there's only so many years in eternity.

Anyway, I find Kris, alone and I walk up to him my eyes searching the empty glass case. "What are we looking at?" I ask, hoping I haven't made a fool of myself by asking the obvious question. I do that sometimes.

"It used to be a key," Kris says. His baritone voice sends chills like the North wind straight to my roots. What a Mythic.

"Key? Where is it?"

"Stolen I suspect."

I looked at him. His usual jolly demeanor was replaced by a serious expression. A frown now creased his forehead.

"Stolen? Why would a Mythic steal anything?" I said.

He shrugged.

My questions were soon answered when the Fairy Godmother burst from her tent at the rear of exhibit and ran to the glass case. I felt for her. I know all about calls of nature.

She pressed her hands on the glass, her eyes frantic. "Oh, my spells! It's gone!"

***

Now, as many of you know Kris is a hero so naturally he volunteered to retrieve the missing key. Like a fool in love-at-first-sight I offered to help in anyway I could. Kris seemed pleased because he winked at me. And not one of those naughty winks either.

Naturally the key is magical. It's called the Sapphire Key.

I know what you're thinking, and you'd be right.

This is one of those stories where if the magic key falls into the wrong hands it's the end of the world. Well, not exactly the world just the mythic world. My world.

Fairy Godmother explained that the key was for a chest of secrets. She also said the secret chest was stolen while in transit to the convention.

The MAC Bureau of Investigation (the MAC BI) suspected the Bogey Man was responsible. But so far they'd been unable to discover any clues linking him to the theft.

Earlier in eternity Bogey was banished to the nether region, for conduct unbecoming a Mythic. It was going to be difficult to prove his involvement. At his sentencing Bogey swore revenge against the entire Mythic world. Unlike the mortal world when a Mythic swears revenge you have to take him seriously.

The big problem was Kris and I would have to face the trial of the Titans to get to the Bogey Man's house in the nether region. From what I hear about the Titans they're temperamental beings who eat kittens and puppies for breakfast.

Well, actually that last part's just a rumor. Unconfirmed.

***

Kris and I set out the next day with the blessing of the President of MAC, Saint Patrick. I'd never met the President before that day. He was taller than I expected, for a leprechaun.

Kris was in the lead with me close behind as we entered the Hairy Hills. So-called because they are covered with long strands of naturally occurring hair. Elves comb them out all day every day. As you can imagine it's hard work to maintain hills with hair. I'd sure hate to get caught in a knot let me tell you.

Today Kris wore a red jumpsuit the same color as his suit from yesterday. He wore polished black boots that gleamed in the sunlight. He was whistling a tune I didn't recognize.

"What's that song?" I asked.

"Oh, something I heard on the radio the other day. Something about tiny flying reindeer and a storm." He shrugged. "It kind of stuck in my head. You know what that's like."

I nodded as my sandals crunched fallen follicles with each step.

"Yes, I do. I can't get a song the Bushmen of the Serengeti sing about me out of my head." He laughed.

This man was my kind of hero. Modest, funny, strong, brave, and beautiful. I had to be the luckiest Mythic in existence to even be on the same hill as a hero like him

After several hours we'd hiked high into hills. It had grown colder with each passing hour. I cinched my robes tighter and Kris had pulled the jumpers hood over his head.

To our surprise we arrived at a precipice. Stretched out ahead of us was a deep chasm. The ledge on the opposite side was at least fifty feet distant. Too far to jump without assistance. We could really have used Kris' tiny flying reindeer right now.

I stood looking into that chasm. I thought about turning back and telling Pat we'd failed. Kris looked around and spotted a stalk of hair thicker than the others that he pointed out to me.

It was thick and at least seventy feet long. If we could get it to lay flat we could use it as a bridge.

"I don't have any hair gel. Sorry," I said.

He laughed. "You're so funny. We don't need gel. What we need is a big wind to blow the hair down across this chasm."

He was right of course. Kris wasn't just a pretty face. He was smart too. And I was falling in love with him.

"No problem." I raised my hands to the sky and commanded the wind to blow from behind the giant stalk of hair. I manipulated the wind as it grew in intensity so that the stalk would fall exactly where I wanted it to land.

Kris had the foresight to grab the nearest stalk and hold tight as the winds power increased.

The roots of the giant stalk tore out of the ground with a loud rip.

The stalk dropped across the chasm just as I'd envisioned. Perfect. Mission accomplished.

I commanded the winds to die down and turned to face Kris with a grin on my face.

"Whew!" he said. "That's some blow."

"Best in the business, Kris."

His laugh thrilled me to my roots.

***

When we arrived on the opposite side of the chasm we were met by the Titan, Cronus.

In ancient times Cronus was the ruler of the Titans and a rather nasty brute. Now he looked like a shriveled old man. He was hunched over and only able to walk with the aid of a twisted wooden cane. And he smelled bad.

His only clothing was what looked like the New Year Baby's hand-me-down diaper only in an adult size. It was a kind of adult diaper. Nasty.

"Hello," said Kris. "I'm Kris Kri —"

"I'm Mother Nature and this is Kris. We're looking for the Bogey Man. Do you know where he lives?"

"What?" said the ancient Titan. "Who're you?"

Great. He's deaf too. I was about to order a lightning bolt to scare the old guy into telling us what we needed to know when Kris intervened.

"Would you like a gift?" he said. Cronus appeared to understand Kris because his dull eyes gleamed with delight.

Kris smiled and reached into a hidden pocket in his coveralls. He pulled out a brand new ivory handled cane made of the finest teak wood I'd ever seen.

I recall wondering how he managed to conceal the cane in his pocket. But the happiness in the old Titan's eyes made me forget about the how's and why's for the moment.

"Will you let us pass? "said Kris.

Cronus smiled and nodded as he accepted the gift. He handed Kris the old cane and pointed to a red brick road that disappeared at the horizon. I assumed the road led to Bogey's house.

Kris winked at me and said, "We're off to see the Bogey Man." He pointed to the road. "Follow the red brick road."

***

Bogey's house was in a deep, dark forest of trees. The red brick road ended at the edge of this dark wood. Since this was the nether world, and I hadn't created these woods, my powers wouldn't work here. Talk about being uncomfortable.

Kris stopped me before the road ended. "I can't let you go there. It's too dangerous," he said.

Unbelievable! Who does he think he's talking to? I'm freakin' Mother Nature! But darned if he wasn't right. Without my powers I was just another Mythic. But if you think I was about to let him go ahead without me then you'd be wrong. We were in this together.

"Kris, I appreciate your concern. It's all very chivalrous, dashing, and heroic of you but I can take care of myself."

Kris smiled and shook his head. "It's not like that, Mother N." He pointed to a piece of ground at the edge of the woods. "Quicksand. We have to go around."

***

Bogey's cottage was right out of the storybooks. Thatched roof, a gunmetal chimney trailing gray smoke, and wood framed windows.

It appeared all very harmless.

Until I noticed the doorknocker was in the shape of a gargoyle. That's how I knew this fairy tale house was the home of the Bogey Man and not some magical princess.

You don't scare me, buddy, I thought, I've scared more butts out of more chairs than you ever will.

Kris stepped up to the door to rap the knocker three times against the heavy oak door. Almost as if he'd been waiting for us, the door swung open and we stood face-to-face with the Bogey Man.

His single blood-shot green eye registered his surprise at seeing us on his doorstep. Around his scaly neck was a pink cloth dinner napkin. In his right hand was a half eaten chicken leg. Other than the napkin all he had on were crimson pajama bottoms dotted with hearts that read, I Love Mom.

Some Mythic beastie. He couldn't scare anyone looking like he did.

"Hi," said Kris. "Mind if we come in?"

"Huh…yeah…sure."

Kris winked that special wink at me again. This caused my heart to flutter. Wow! What a hottie!

The inside of Bogey's house looked like one of my patented tornadoes had ripped though the place. Newspapers littered the floor. Every end table and the coffee table had dirty dishes stacked up in uneven piles. Moldy food had been left on the plates. Out of the corner of one eye I spotted a mouse scurry over the stained grey carpet.

Bogey was definitely a bachelor.

"Have you seen the Sapphire Key?" said Kris. There was no beating around the bush with this guy. Cool.

Bogey shook his head in bewilderment. "The what?"

Kris nodded. "As I thought." He turned and started for the door.

"Hey, Kris, wait," I said. He stopped and turned to look at me.

There was a mischievous glint in his eye. Quite fetching actually. "You believe him? Look at him. He's the Bogey Man!"

"I know he's the Bogey Man, but no one ever lies to me." With that he walked out the front door.

I looked at Bogey. "Is he for real?" Bogey shrugged.

I ran after Kris and caught up with him on the red brick road. "Kris! Hold up."

He stopped and faced me. "So where is the Sapphire Key?" I asked.

He shrugged. "At the convention exhibit hall I assume."

"What? How can that be?"

"The key and the secret chest are invisible."

***

Sure enough Kris was right. When we arrived back at the convention we found an apologetic Fairy Godmother. Apparently she'd used an invisibility spell as a security measure to protect the chest and the key from thieves. But she forgot about it.

There was relief all round. Especially by the MAC BI special agent who agreed not to file mischief charges against the Fairy Godmother.

"All's well that ends well," said Kris.

The rest of the convention went well until finally it was time for my keynote address to the attendees. I took the opportunity to announce my retirement, and to announce my engagement to Kris Kringle.

I was going to marry a real hero. My hero.

***

So that's the story of how I became Mrs. Santa Claus. Sounds like one of those fairy tale endings doesn't it? Of course you ask what possible problem could I have being married to a hero like Kris? After all he's a hero to the whole world.

It turns out under the rules set down in the by-laws of the MAC and CHEESE Kris is only allowed to be a hero for one day a year. And which day do you think he ends up choosing every year? Christmas day of course!

And those tiny flying reindeer? Well…don't get me started.

The Penguin Sleeps With The Fishes
A Yellow & Bird Mystery

FROM MY PERCH I WATCHED FRANK'S FACE in the mirror over the cheaply made veneer dresser. The dresser was pushed against the wall at the end of the bed of our rent-by-the-hour hotel room. He carefully shaved the two day's worth of grey and black stubble off his product-of-the-mean-streets puss. In between strokes of the straight razor he wiped the edge of the blade on a faded grey towel, placed next to the aluminum bowl. The surface of the water in the bowel was shiny with oily soap. A smoldering Camel, stuck from the side of his cruel mouth, made me cough. The cigarette was stinking up my air.

I shuffled down the wooden perch closer to the window and wished for the tenth time, in the past fifteen minutes, it was open. But for the tenth time it was still nailed shut. I sighed. The things I'll sacrifice for the good of our partnership. Clean air was the least of our troubles.

Good thing the window was closed actually. The summer San Francisco air outside was just above freezing. My tail feathers will freeze in ten seconds. Parrots aren't built for this kind of weather.

The only radio station in town predicted a high of forty today, but I doubted it, not with an iceberg in the harbor.

"You say sumthin', Bird?" Frank mumbled. He leaned closer to his reflection to examine his image. He squinted, swiped the blade over his face, then snorted with satisfaction. He had scraped away the last of the dark hairs with the razor.

"Naw, nunthin', Frank, just thought—"

The rotary dial phone affixed to a bracket on the of the walls covered with faded wallpaper rang. The receiver rattled in the cradle.

"Ouch!" Frank nicked his chin.

A dot of blood appeared where the scar from Oscar Ruiz's knife still showed on his chin. Old Oscar was dumb that day. Never bring a knife to a gunfight are words I live by, and Oscar died by. Guy was good with a knife though; he had left his mark on my partner of fifteen years, before his timecard was punched for good.

I left my perch and flew to the phone. I snatched the receiver from the cradle in my left claw, then carried it back to my perch. That extra long extension cord, installed last month, really worked well. While balanced on one foot, I raised the receiver to my beak.

"FYI. Bird speaking." Even in the bad times it's good business to be polite when answering the phone. Parrots are polite.

"Bird? It's Chief. We got trouble."

I love that word. Whenever I hear the word trouble I smell a hundred a day, plus expenses.

"Yeah, Chief. What is it this week? Flaming arrows the size of Cadillac's? A flying saucer flown by a cockroach from the planet Ick who speaks five languages? Or maybe another iceberg in the harbor?"

"Enough with the jokes, Bird. This is serious. This time it's murder."

I whistled. In the mirror I saw Frank cock an eyebrow. He was busy dabbing the cut on his chin with a wad of toilet paper. I lowered the receiver from my beak and whispered, "A real case, Frank!"

If I had opposing thumbs I would have given him a thumbs up. Instead all I could do was flap my left wing. A grin spread over his swarthy features.

"Are you talkin' to Yellow?"

"Uhhh, yeah, sorry, Chief. He's right here. Wanta talk to him?"

"Nope. All I want is you to get your feathery butt to Fisherman's Wharf, Pier 47 A-SAP. And bring Frank with ya."

Curiosity was eating me up inside. "So...who's dead?"

"Peter Penguin." The line went dead.

I stared at the receiver for several seconds, too stunned to speak.

Frank had donned his favorite powder blue dress shirt, but hadn't buttoned it yet. He was picking out a matching tie, from the three hung on a wire coat hanger in the closet, beside his two suits. My silence stopped him. He glanced over his shoulder at me. Silence is not a parrot trait, so my quiet was deafening.

He turned away from the closet and frowned. "What gives, Bird?"

I found my voice again. "The Penguin sleeps with the fishes."

***

I wasn't surprised Peter Penguin was dead.

It seemed everyone on the planet wanted him dead these days. Penguin was at the epicenter of a promotional campaign of hate, revenge, and disembowelment. During a LOX News Network Special Report, When Scientists Kill, the United States Attorney General herself announced a bounty on Penguin's head. The bounty would make someone the richest person in the world. Well, the richest for a year...at least. I hope.

And in an article in Armageddon Monthly, an e-mag I subscribe to, the President, from the Oval Office at Puerto Rico White House, was quoted as saying, "Someone must kill this man."

Odd thing to say for such a nice guy as the President, but doomsday had made everyone jumpy, me included. As it turned out talk was cheap.

Now he had been murdered, and the possible suspects numbered in the billions. How were we ever going to find a killer in this haystack? It was like a broken pencil to speculate...pointless.

When the reason behind the world's poles shifting was discovered, and Dr. Penguin's Doomsday machine came to light, the doc disappeared into a rabbit hole. No one had seen him since, until today.

Our involvement was simple. Ruby, Penguin's wife, is Franks ex. I was her pet parrot, until she tossed both is us over for the fame and fortune of being married to a Nobel Prize winning egghead.

"Do you think Ruby'll be happy to see you?" Frank grunted in reply.

We stood shivering on the sidewalk in an icy wind, waiting for a taxicab.

I was perched on the padded right shoulder of his double-breasted, navy blue, pinstriped suit. My wings were folded in front of my body, to provide some insulation.

The black and white Ford Whisper taxicab appeared from around the corner. The cab stopped next to the curb. The cab driver was one of those grizzled veterans of the fare wars, hunchbacked, with grey stubble that covered his leathery face, like a worn rug. He grunted, "Where to?" once Frank and I were seated in the rear compartment.

"Pier 47," I said.

The driver's beady eyes narrowed at Frank in the rear view. Frank nodded.

The driver shrugged, grunted again, then the cab pulled away from the curb smooth and noiselessly. Electric cars are quiet. Kind of eerie in way, but who doesn't want to help protect the environment, even this close to the end of the world?

Bulletproof glass separated us from the driver, and gave us privacy. No use in setting off the celebration too soon by letting our renta-chaufer in on the good news. Ding-dong the Penguins dead, would scream from the headlines soon enough.

We didn't talk about the case anyway, just in case the driver had a mini-recorder installed to pick up some juicy gossip he could sell to the National Tattletale. Loose lips make cabbies rich.

Traffic was light. In less than fifteen minute we turned off Powell onto Jefferson, and parked at the entrance to Pier 47.

Once the car stopped Frank got out, with me still perched on his shoulder.

Frank reached in his pants pocket and pulled out his billfold, held together by a solid silver clip, a wedding gift from his ex. He peeled off a twenty and stuck it through the small opening in the driver's window.

"Keep the change, driver." Frank smiled at me. "Courtesy of Frank Yellow Investigations." Frank handed the driver an F.Y.I business card.

The driver accepted the card and shrugged. Frank tipped the brim of his fedora and turned to walk away. I looked back as we walked away, and saw the business card flutter into the gutter, then the taxi sped away.

"Ya know, Frank, the fare was only a sawbuck. And I've been eating a lot of budgie seed lately."

Frank nodded. "Yeah, I know. The cabbie may need our services some day. Think of it as a promotional expense."

I pictured the image of our business card landing in the icy gutter.

"Yeah. OK." Frank never could read people very well, but then the detecting part of our partnership was my job.

As we approached the arch over the entrance to Pier 47 two penguins greeted us. There was the irony of penguins living in San Francisco, where Peter Penguin's body turned up, but they were illegal aliens, and Peter Penguin was a citizen.

Penguin is not one of my languages so we steered well clear as we walked under the arch and onto the deserted pier. Good thing too, because the smell of dead fish was thick even at this distance. Personally, I've never understood eating anything except seed, but what do I know? Parrots aren't gourmet cooks.

The Chief appeared down the pier. He wagged his tail when he spotted us. "Over here, Bird...Yellow!"

The coroner, Lars Pederson, appeared from a doorway.

His normally pale cheeks were rosy from the cold, and the hood of his parka was pulled over his short blond hair. Frank quickened his pace and we hurried past darkened t-shirt, jewellery, and souvenir stores. The shop owners had left San Francisco long ago. What creeped me out was the shops were still stocked, as if the people had suddenly disappeared. The world had become one of those B grade science fiction movies. Only this wasn't a movie, this was real.

I stayed in San Francisco because it's my home, and Frank needs me. Besides where am I going to go?

Lars took Frank's hand in his, he shook it vigorously. If you didn't know them you would have thought they were just trying to keep warm, but the two men had been friends back to their days at PS 32, in Brooklyn. They launched into one of those let's-catch-up conversations.

"Polly want a cracker?" I looked down to see Chief next to Lars. Chief was a five-year old Jack Russell terrier. He's a small dog with a big chip on his shoulder. Trouble with a capital T. I rolled my eyes.

"Very funny, Chief."

Chief laughed gruffly. Some things never change. "Where's the body?"

Chief nosed Lars' left leg. "Lars, show Yellow and Bird our victim."

I didn't like the tongue in cheek quality to his tone. After all a man had been murdered, and the killer was still on the loose.

What kind of leg humper are you, Chief?

Lars nodded, then he led us into the store he'd just come from. It was a movie memorabilia store. The walls were covered with movies posters, and there were racks of DVD's. Glass stands, that contained rows of action figures and celebrity bobble heads, lined both walls. Everything was covered with a layer of dust, and the floor was covered in sand. Without the sand the wooden planking would have been a skating rink.

Only this ice smelled like wet corpse.

Lars led the way to the back of the store. Behind a counter, where I presume the cashier used to stand, though the cash register had been removed, leaving behind ragged holes where the register had once been was the body of the late Professor Penguin.

He lay spread eagled on his back, his face the color of chalk, his bloodless lips blue. He was dressed in a tuxedo. Hmmm...a penguin in a penguin suit. Irony had reached new heights.

In the center of his chest, about where his heart was, was a dark round hole, obviously the entry point of the bullet that killed him. Good shootin', tex..._

Frank dropped to his haunches, and flicked his fedora back on his forehead with his index finger. I flew to the counter to land near the edge. I wanted a bird's eye view of the crime scene.

"How long has he been dead?" I asked.

"Don't know, Bird," answered Lars.

33

I turned my head so one eye faced the lanky coroner. "Why not?"

He shrugged. "He's been in the water too long."

"Water? What are you talkin' about, Lars? He's in here, not in the bay." I glanced at Frank. He regarded me with an annoyed look in his eyes. Frank was right. Something's fishy, and it's not the penguins by the entrance to the pier.

"Ok...Chief what's this all about?" Frank stood and glared at the terrier. The cops in this town had gone to the dogs.

"We were hopin' you guys would know." Chief's gruff voice was even, and his eyes were serious.

Thanks, Chief, you just threw me a bone. "He means he thinks we plugged the Penguin, Frank."

Frank smirked. "Com'on, Chief. We're law abiding citizens. You know that."

Chief's eyes sagged and he sat back onto his haunches. "You're right, of course. But I'm baffled. The clothing and the body are soaked in salt water, but we found him in here. We're stumped."

"Who called it in?" I asked.

"A woman. She didn't leave her name. We traced the call to a phone booth on Clay Street. Nothing."

My brow wrinkled. "Was there any identification on the body?"

Chief looked at me with that are-you-pulling-my-hind-leg expression. Yeah, everyone on the planet knows Peter Penguin on site.

"No." It was Lars who spoke this time. "But we did find this..."

He handed me a plasticized business card. It read, Madame Ybur, palm reader, medium. Odd name. Must be Iraqi. "Mind if I keep this?"

The address on the card was on Kearney, not far from Clay. The madam's name twigged something in my memory.

Chief nodded. "Sure. We already checked it out. The old lady is goofy, but not goofy enough to kill anyone."

"Thanks." I gave the card to Frank who pocketed it. Parrots don't have pockets.

We said our goodbyes and started to walk back to the street. Along the way Frank lit a cigarette. I rolled my eyes as the acrid smoke wafted over me. "When are going to give those up? They'll kill you."

Frank snorted. "What difference does it make now?"

He had a point. "But if that were true, Frank then we may as well lay down right now and die. Remember, we're trying to solve a murder because we want to, not because we have to. There's a big difference."

I shifted tactics. "Frank, what if you were with Ruby again? She hated when you smoked."

Frank shrugged as he took a long drag from the Camel before answering. "Yeah, you're right. I guess I'd quit." He chuckled. "But that's not going to happen, Bird. You can bet your yellow and green butt on that."

"I'm not so sure about that."

***

We arrived in the same taxi as the one that had dropped us off at Pier 47. The driver was the same. And he had the same dislike for customers. Frank acted like they were old friends.

We arrived at the address in a few minutes. When we got out the driver seemed to drive away faster than the first time. Fifteen dollar tips don't buy what they used to. It didn't help that Frank had to pay him with a combination of dollar bills and quarters, and the tip was only twenty-five cents.

I rolled my eyes at Frank. He blushed. Big man, throwing around fat cash as if we had any. "Let's find Madame Ybur. I need a drink so I want to get to the nearest watering hole as soon as possible."

Frank and I entered through the revolving glass doors to the lobby. The lobby was a combination of smoked glass, gleaming chrome, and marble, In the middle of the lobby was a wide pond. A tall palm tree, heavy with coconuts, sprouted from amongst a jungle of smaller plants on an artificial island in the center of the pond. Beautiful.

In one corner of the lobby was a kiosk, like the ones at the mall. Only this kiosk didn't sell knock off watches, or Japanese animé action figures. This kiosk was for matters related to the occult, palm reading, and a medium who would contact your loved ones on the other side. Given recent developments a medium might be a useful skill, if it wasn't a scam.

Next to the kiosk, sitting on a wooden stool, was a dark haired woman dressed as a gypsy. Business was slow so she had her eyes buried in a novel. It must have been a good book because she didn't look up until we were stood over her. From my perch on Frank's shoulder I could see the book was a romance.

She looked up into Frank's eyes and the initial surprise was quickly replaced by joy. Her look was enough to warm the cuckolds of my heart. If I was human. But I'm a parrot, we have different tastes.

"Madame Ybur?" I asked from my perch.

Madame Ybur laughed. What did I say that was so funny? "Sorry. It's just funny to hear you say my name backwards."

Backwards? Ruby! Ruby...Peter's wife...Frank's ex-wife...Peter Penguin's dead...Frank...Ruby...oh, oh...

Before I could stop them, I was forced to fly off Frank's shoulder as Ruby and Frank rushed at each other. They locked in a passionate embrace. They're lips were glued to each other's and their arms were wrapped around each other bodies. No doubt the only thing that would separate them now was a fire hose on full blast.

Since I wasn't about to do that that I flew to the kiosk and landed. I folded my wings and waited.

Looking around the kiosk I saw the typical trappings of the paranormal huckster.

Books on metaphysics, crystals in various shapes, baby food-sized jars that contained a rainbow of colored powders. It was a real fraud-fest. And with the bunko squad on permanent vacation Ruby was going to be successful with her fraud. Not that it mattered. Doomsday was just around the corner.

Then, of course there was the murder of Peter Penguin. I spotted the butt of a gun sticking from under a sheet of paper on the kiosk's counter top. And next to the gun was a voodoo doll with pins sticking from the center of its chest.

As I suspected Ruby, who spelled her name backwards for the purpose marketing her disguise as a tarot card reader, murdered her husband.

My problem now was do I ruin what's left of Frank's life and turn her in, or do I ignore his happiness and call Chief?

I made up my mind immediately. At least Frank will stop smoking.

The things I'll sacrifice for the good of our partnership, and our friendship.

It was the end of the world as we know it, but love would endure forever. And I'll be breathing clean air. Besides I'm a parrot not a stool pigeon.

Sorry, Chief.

The Eliminators

"Impossible..." I breathed.

The rapid beating of my heart eclipsed the incessant growl of big city traffic coming from the street below the office window.

It — the spectral figure — levitated a meter above the scored and heavily traveled hardwood floor of our cramped, dusty office.

We're located in a two-story walk up, near the corner of Main and Hastings Streets on the east side of Vancouver. Harry and I have operated our PI business from the 50-year-old-plus office building for the past five years. I sometimes forget five years has passed since we'd opened The Eliminators Paranormal Investigative Service together as partners. Most people called us The Eliminators for short. (I certainly prefer this over the unflattering E-PIS our detractors call us.)

The truth was we were secretly under contract to the City of Vancouver's finest. Not that the VPD chief would ever admit we often worked for the cops when they were faced with unexplained paranormal crime. The chief's office was just two blocks from where I stood yet he had never even set foot inside our door.

His kiss-ass assistant, Blake "Blakey" Thomas acted as his intermediary. Blakey is such a weasel.

The press dubs us the Ghostbusters named I suppose after that Dan Ackroyd movie in the eighties. In reality, we had never seen an actual ghost until this moment. And the one standing before me looked very much like my mother.

I shivered in the cold air. Unusual for an August afternoon when the outside temperature neared forty degrees Celsius, and normally even warmer in here.

The woman-shaped phantom stood, or should I say floated, on the opposite side of my scarred forties era pine desk indeed looked the spitting image of my mother. Expect for the dark pupiless eyes she could easily pass as Mom's doppelganger. A twin maybe. A dead twin perhaps, but still a mirror image of my mother.

Not that I knew if dear old Mom was alive, or dead. I hadn't seen her in a <u>long</u> time.

Dressed in tan walking shorts, a mustard yellow sleeveless tee shirt, and brown leather sandals Mom's gaze was unflinchingly fixed on me. Her ensemble must be all the rage amongst the best-dressed ghosts these days.

"Huh…what…what…do you want…" I managed to stammer from between frozen lips. The sweetened coffee I had been sipping turned sour in my mouth.

Out of the corner of one eye I saw my partner Harry — only the scuffed soles of his brown leather shoes were visible — his tree trunk like legs were crossed atop his equally ancient desk. His muscular fingers were laced across his wide chest and his cool blue eyes were fixated on the ghost. That was Harry. Cool as the proverbial cucumber.

He had been in the process of writing up the invoice for our latest client when the ghost suddenly appeared.

Mr. Wallace hired us to follow his wife, who he thought was unfaithful. For this one we didn't even have to leave the office. Easy money.

Harry's gift for foretelling the future meant he had seen Mrs. Wallace's lover's death in a seven-car pile up on Route One. It was going to rain hard the next day and Harry saw the guy's green Dodge Ram roll over and burst into flames. The guy was barbecue.

An ugly scene true, but it meant some much funds would join their meager cousins in the bank.

Poor Harry. He didn't much care for his so-called "gift" in cases like the guy with the truck. I had to agree seeing and feeling the guy's terror as he burned to death was not much of gift.

Though he is able to see future events he is unable to change them in any way. If he saw the country was about to be nuked he would be helpless to stop it. Sure, he could warn people, and leave the country himself, but the nukes would still fall. Talk about the ultimate raw deal.

Me? I can move stuff with my mind. I always figured that's why Mom left us, and Dad drank himself to death. They just couldn't handle my gift.

In the Wallace's case, Mrs. Wallace would not be cheating with that guy again. And she wouldn't cheat with anyone else. Harry had seen that as well.

I offered my opinion that Mrs. Wallace must have really loved the guy — the lover, not the husband — Harry wasn't so sure.

He thought Mrs. Wallace was damned scared of what might happen to her. She suspected her husband was behind the accident. Kinda like that Harrison Ford movie, about a lawyer whose wife murders his mistress. Being in the PI business means you encounter a lot of loonies.

For five years we had been at this location, and for five years we have been trying, without success, to move The Eliminators Paranormal Investigative Service up the PI food chain. We were eager to get closer to the really big bucks downtown. Simple really. If only we could snag one of those upscale clients — and if the press stopped calling us a couple of nuts — then we might stand a real chance at success.

The slumlord that ran this two-story walk-up demanded more rent every year. This meant we had less and less for the luxuries, like food.

"You can't be my mother," I said to the silent apparition. "I haven't seen her in fifteen years. Nor do I want to. Ever."

To emphasize my point I used my telekinesis to fly a white china coffee cup off the makeshift shelf I had installed over the drip coffee pot directly at its head. It passed through her then shattered with a loud bang against the opposite wall, near the sagging gray metal file cabinet.

Harry sighed. "Do ya really have to do that?"

"Sorry. I — "

"You have to kill me," said the ghost suddenly. Her voice was soft and echoed as if she were speaking from inside a steel drum.

Harry suddenly fell backward to land with a loud bang against the cheap tile floor. "Oh. My. God," he said.

A shiver ran through me. Harry knew something. His gift was telling him something--something bad. His face was pale; as pale as the white dress shirt he wore under his smoke-gray suit jacket. I hated his ties, but never said so to his face anyway. This one was a ghastly flora pattern

Do something, numb nuts, I said to myself. But it was as if I were frozen where I stood. Fear gripped me and my limbs refused to respond to my brains instructions.

I detected a faint odor of ozone in the air. It was as if an electrical charge surrounded the ghost of my mother. This is too weird.

"My son was always useless," she said.

I didn't have to listen to this crap. Before I could stop myself years of pent up frustration and anger spilled out of me. "You ran out on us, Dad was devastated — I was only twelve."

"All true. But you don't know the whole truth." The ghost of Mary Alice O'Shay turned to face me. "Your father beat me, or had your forgotten about that part of our happy home life."

I felt my ears grow warm. "No. But Dad had—issues."

"Dad was a drunk." She snorted in disgust.

Now as I said, Harry and I had never seen a real ghost before. We had certainly uncovered a few frauds, but this spirit didn't look like faked special effects. Not, like the case Harry and I solved when the disgraced special effects guy used SFX to scare a widow out of her family fortune.

He'd blackmailed her by haunting her with her deceased husbands ghost. The "ghost" said she had murdered him for his money. All true of course, she had certainly murdered her husband ten years before. But, the special effects guy just could not resist the urge to use his talents to fool the old lady. Scared her to death. Heart attack.

We caught the special effects guy the old-fashioned way. Too bad really. At the time, I thought it would be nice to see the ghost of her dead husband. Now I wasn't so certain.

"Huh, Jimmy..."said Harry. "I don't wanta interrupt your family reunion, but it seems to me we have a larger issue here. Like why is a ghost standing in our office?"

Mary chuckled. "Of course. Harry's right. James, you and I will have to work through this baggage of ours later. Besides, there isn't a lot of time."

"For what?" I said. My eyes narrowed, while my voice echoed my suspicion.

"Like I started to say, before we began our trip down memory lane, you have to kill me. Within the next hour," she said. The way she said the words, they seemed so matter-of-fact, it sent a chill through me.

If she needed to die then that was one thing. The far greater problem was how do you kill someone who is already dead?

***

Over the years, Harry and I have seen a lot of strange things. If people knew there were vampires, werewolves, monsters of every shape and kind, and aliens from planets too distant to be seen by Hubble, walking among them they would freak. But the ghost of my dead mother? That definitely ranked highest on my strange scale.

And, it got even stranger when Mary explained she was the ghost of her future self. Twenty years in the future to be exact. She apparently died after being in a coma for twenty years. A coma caused by being hit by a car, today.

Somehow, I would kill her so she wouldn't have to spend the next twenty years in a coma before she succumbed.

My head hurt. "Nope. I don't think so, Mom. Besides, why should I help you? I don't even like you!"

Mary hung her head. "Tell him, Harry."

Harry dropped his shoes to the floor with thump. The odor of disturbed dust permeated the air. "She's right Jimmy. She will be hit by the car today and be in the coma for twenty years…"

I felt Mary's dark eyes gazing at me. "Son. James. I am still your mother. I love you. I know I haven't been there for you for a long time."

44

Her voice was gentle, enveloping me with its soft summer breeze quality.

"You bet your ass," I said. Even as I said the words, I knew I was being too harsh. What galled me most was she was right.

When I first met Harry in grade ten, at John Oliver Secondary, he told me my whole life story in ten minutes. It was as if the guy worked for Sixty Minutes. Now here was my mother's damn ghost confirming my best friend's twisted tale. Harry warned me would be days like this. And Harry is never wrong.

"I'm so sorry, James. Sorry I wasn't there. Sorry I..." She paused. "I'm going to be hit by a car today. Then I'll be in a coma for the next twenty years before I die. The police will track you down as my only living relative, and you're going to tell them not to pull the plug on me. You're so consumed with guilt that you just can't let me go. I don't want you to go through that, son."

I glared at Harry whose face was a shade of pink. He had never told me this about my mother. What good was a guy who left out the most important parts about a guy's mother? The messy bits I call them.

He shrugged his broad shoulders. "Hey. Don't look at me. Sure I saw her accident, and the coma thingy, but I thought you didn't wanta see her. I mean you always say..."

"Never mind." I cut him off. "We'll talk about this later."

Mary's ghost floated to the window over looking the late morning traffic. Cars honked their horns and trucks rumbled by below our window. The odor of burnt gasoline wafted in from the street. She gazed into the street with a longing I had had never seen in a living person, never mind a dead one.

Her voice became small. "I don't want to live the next twenty years of my earthly existence in a useless husk." She whirled to face me her expression grim.

"You have to kill me."

What could I do? Harry said the car would hit her, and she is — or rather was — oh shit — my head was spinning. I nodded. "Yeah, I guess so."

"Whoa," Hal said holding his hands up as if he were surrendering to Castro's army. "You might be charged with murder. You can't just go around killing people ya know. Besides we don't know where Mary is right now."

I shot him a warning look. "Don't you start with me." I knew perfectly well that if I were going to be caught Harry would know already. And somehow I knew that he knew I wouldn't be caught. (This stuff is just too weird for words.) He'd already seen it. Good thing neither of us have criminal minds. If we did we'd make a killing on horseracing or at the casinos. Honesty really does have its drawbacks.

Mary's ghost pointed out the window to the busy street. I moved to look where Mary was pointing. Sure enough, there walking down the cracked sidewalk, was the very much alive Mary O'Shay, the former Mrs. Ivan Rusinski.

Harry and I looked at each other. He wore a stunned expressions on his faces which I'm sure mirrored my own. My mother had been this close to me and I had never even realized it.

I stood straight and looked at my partner. "So, Harry, how do I kill her?"

***

Mary's ghost told me she was only visible to Harry and I. And that she could have be visible to anyone she wanted to see her. She didn't want anyone else to see her but us at the moment. Strange how the rules of the paranormal so often turn out to be so simple.

46

Even more strange was that in some sort of cosmic joke if we succeeded then a woman would be murdered — this was really, really crazy.

We rode in silence in my '82 Buick. Mary sat — if that's what ghosts do — in the back seat gazing around at the city that flashed by.

"I remember how this looked." An occasional glance in the rear view told me she was taking everything in with her strange eye as we neared the suburb of New Westminster. The sparkling neon signs of the movie and entertainment complex known as Metropolis were behind us.

Mary's eyes were as wide as a child's as we passed the massive entertainment complex. "I don't remember this," she said in a tiny voice

Our destination beyond New West is Surrey.

It was nearly noon and the sun had warmed the inside of the ancient Buick. The faux leather seats stuck to my pants. I wasn't sure if it was the heat, or my nerves, making me sweat so profusely.

We arrive to find the sky train parking lot is packed with cars. Not unusual at this time of day since the lot is for downtown commuters who save money by parking their cars here then ride the rapid transit service to the downtown business district.

The parking lots were well known to cops and crooks alike as the car thief strip mall. Every make and model of car and truck imaginable was lined up in neat rows ready for inspection by their new "owners".

When we arrived, we saw the bike patrol cop in her lemon yellow vest, with the word 'POLICE' in bold black lettering on the back, pedaling away on her taxpayer funded thousand dollar mountain bike. Perfect timing.

She didn't give us a second glance as she went by. Two guys in suits — regardless if the suits looked like their owners had slept in them — certainly weren't your usual car thief type.

In normal circumstances she'd be right. Then these were far from normal circumstances.

We drove slowly through the parking lot until we found an older model Toyota with button locks. It would be the easiest to steal.

I stepped out and used my telekinesis to unlock the driver's door. As I did so, Harry slid behind the wheel of the Buick.

Harry his pale forehead beaded with sweat motioned for me to hurry. His bloodless knuckles gripped the steering wheel. I had never seen him like this. His body trembled with nerves as he kneaded the plastic wheel as if he were making bread dough. My normally cool partner was scared. To tell the truth so was I.

The door squealed metal-on-metal as I opened it. Harry squeezed his eyes tight. Damn!

I quickly sat behind the wheel and went to work on the steering column. I had stolen a couple of cars in my impetuous youth so I certainly knew how.

The plastic cover over the steering column came off easily and I managed to find the wires. I cut them with the box cutter I brought with me. I striped the wires and crossed them correctly. I twisted the yellow and blue wires together then brought the green and white wires together to create the spark to kick over the starter motor.

Nothing. No spark.

Beads of sweat formed on my brow, and dripped into my eyes, blinding me. I tried again. Nothing. I slammed the dashboard hard in frustration with my fist. Deciding I had wasted too much time I stepped out then realized the dashboard didn't look right. Someone had installed an after factory immobilizer.

I shook my head and silently chastised myself.

"What's the matter," said Harry, his voice an urgent whisper.

"Immobilizer. We have to find another car."

We started to cruise the lot again and quickly found an even older car. It was pale green '72 Impala. Harry knew it because he'd owned one just like it in the late seventies.

A pig on gas, but it would more than do the job. The big V8 and the heavy steel body made it the perfect weapon.

***

Once back downtown, Mary directed us to the street she would be on this time of day. It was in Gastown, a tourist area of restored brick buildings and cobblestone streets named after Gassy Jack, a nineteenth century bar owner and local rascal.

In the center of the area was an old steam clock. The cobblestones made for a bumpy ride, but the tourists thought the streets were quaint. To me it was just a jarring joyless ride for the spine.

As we bumped over the worn cobblestones my teeth rattled. Just great.

Harry parked the old Buick, now officially dubbed the "getaway car", on a side street while I would drive the Impala to the spot where Mary was going to be (at least according to our time traveling ghost).

I would use the heavy car run her down and kill her. I was to make sure she was dead by backing up and running over her again.

We knew we'd be changing history, at least Mary's personal history. Of course, the history of the man who'd originally run her down would also be altered, in his case for the better.

What we knew for sure is a car would strike Mary; nothing could change that one fact. It might not be today, but it would happen. And, she'd be in a coma if I didn't help her. To avoid countless years of silent suffering she would die today by my hand.

I shook my head. I now knew what it felt to be Harry and I hated the pain in my belly. But I knew what I had to do. She'd begged me. And even after years of estrangement she was still my mother.

Our plan meant I would abandon the Impala in an alley and escape in the Buick. Hopefully we would get away before anyone would identify us.

"Gotta do it fast," Mary said. "Like Al Pacino in the first Godfather movie when he shoots the gangster and the dirty cop."

Harry and I had forgone the usual PI baggy suits and ties, instead preferring to don jeans and tee shirts. In addition I had added a New York Yankees ball cap and mirrored sunglasses. Harry, the Mr. GQ of our little firm, hated the disguises, but it would lessen the chances of being identified.

As I sat in the Impala I felt my stomach churn. A trace of bile invaded my mouth when I spotted the very much alive Mary O'Shay coming down the sidewalk toward me.

She looked happy. Doubt nearly forced me from the car to warn her about the other guy. But a greater fear of my own failure kept me glued to the seat. Harry said the accident was going to happen no matter what I did.

Mary would either die or be in a coma. What kind of choices were these? Why couldn't I just hit the guy who would hit her, and save her from the coma?

Harry said the only thing we could change was the time of Mary's accident, not the inevitability of it. Harry is always right.

My hands worried the steering wheel until I thought the pale green plastic would come off on my hands.

The vision of her struck by the car became suddenly very clear in my mind. The scream. The blood. The sickening smack of her lifeless body hitting the pavement.

I closed my eyes and struggled to push the sight and sounds of what was about to happen from my mind. And there was something else…

My eyes popped open as the passenger door flew open. It was Harry. "I'm with you, buddy."

"I know," I said. "Let's go."

The Impala moved easily into traffic. As I neared the crosswalk, I picked up speed. The cobblestones made the car bounce into the air as if it wanted to leave the ground.

The powerful engine roared and the wind rushed in through the open windows as we hurled toward my mother. There she was frozen at the sight of the roaring pride of General Motors racing full speed toward her.

I closed my eyes and hit the accelerator hard. Harry screamed. I heard the slap of flesh landing hard as it pounded over the windshield of the car followed by the screams of people on the street around us.

It happened so quickly I thought for a second I might have missed her, until I opened my eyes to glance in the rearview mirror. My heart leapt into my throat.

Framed by the mirror, in the middle of the street behind us, lay a crumpled human form. With both feet I slammed the brake pedal hard causing us to be thrown violently forward. The air filled with the smell of burnt rubber and the screeched of tires as we came to a stop. The seat belt holding me pressed against me until it hurt my chest.

I hit the shift lever into reverse then stepped hard on the accelerator. The car raced backward over the prone lump lying in the middle of the street. It felt like we had hit a speed bump.

I stopped again, shifted into drive, then drove over the body for the last time and headed away. Out of the corner of one eye, I saw the shocked looks of the people watching the horrific spectacle.

Oh, my God. What have I done!

I steered the heavy car around a corner and then into a deserted alley. I felt as if I were moving in thick air as we climbed out of the car leaving the doors open and ran headlong down the dank, dirty alley. The sour smell of garbage, coming from the rusted steel dumpsters that lined the alley, assaulted my senses as we ran. Hot tears streamed down my cheeks.

I killed my own mother!

After what seemed like an eternity, we made it to the Buick, and I threw my sunglasses to the street. Once inside Harry started, the car and we sped away.

He quickly reduced speed as cop cars and an ambulance screamed passed us, going in the opposite direction.

I glanced at Harry, tears blurring eyes that brimmed over with regret and grief. He shook his head sadly and I knew she was dead. I have not seen her for fifteen years and now she was dead.

I heard a soft voice behind me say, "It's okay, son. I know you love me."

***

The headline in the paper the next day stated a stolen car had killed an unidentified pedestrian in a cross walk in Gastown. It was labeled a hit-and-run by the cops, probably — or so the reporter presumed, by kid's joy riding. The cops said they would catch the culprits very soon. The article ended by saying the victims name would not be released until the next of kin were contacted. Of course I already knew the name.

Rain pelted the windows and the smell of fresh coffee permeated the tiny office. Harry's dark eyes, his long legs crossed rested on his desk, were the saddest I had ever seen them. I felt numb.

"I guess Blakey's gonna be calling," murmured Harry.

"Yeah. I guess so."

"What we gonna tell him?"

I shrugged my shoulders. I had no idea. "If he asks we'll tell him we were at a funeral."

"Yeah…" There was nothing else to say.

For several minutes the only sounds in our office came from the incessant ticking of the plastic battery operated clock that hung off the wall. Finally, Harry said, "Where's the ghost?"

I sighed then lifted my coffee mug with the Disney characters dancing happily across it to my lips. "She said she had to do something. But that she'd be here."

The room grew cold. "Hi, boys," said a cheery voice. Too cheery for a dead person in my reckoning.

"What the hell are you so happy about?" I said my voice as bitter as the overcooked coffee.

Mary chuckled. "I'm staying. I have permission."

I moved my legs off my desk and sat forward in my chair my hands gripping the arms of my chair. "What the hell are you talking about?" I said.

"I'm your new partner. I'm going to work cases with you boys." Harry shook his head and snorted.

I thought about asking her who gave her permission, then decided against it. I didn't want to know.

This turn of events pretty much confirmed it: we are officially the strangest PI firm on the planet.

With Death You Get the Eggroll

I HAD JUST PARKED MY RUSTING LOTUS in front of the Ye Olde Dragon's Guild Building — my PI office is on the sixth floor of a four-story walk-up (don't ask, you don't wanta know) — when my cell phone erupted with the deep south standard, Dixie.

I immediately recognized the number on the glowing call display. Why was Owlen calling me from his cell already?

I flipped my phone open. "Where are you?"

"At the corporate headquarters of Y. O. Fortunate Message…"

I knew them. They made the little messages that went into the fortune cookies.

"We found their Vice-President of Sorcery face down in his Won-ton soup…" As usual Owlen used his best dull-investigator voice.

"Accidental drowning?"

"I dun' wanta say any more over an open phone line." The line went dead.

Owlen doesn't share my bent sense of humor. "Yeah. I'll be there in twenty," I said to myself.

I was ten minutes from resting my weary head on the pillow at the end of my ancient overstuffed couch, but now Owlen Vay had sabotaged my perfect plan. There'd be no rest for the wicked this night.

I pushed my frustration and overtired attitude deeper into my guts twisted by too much bad coffee over the last three days and nights. I knew I should have listened to the little voice inside my head whispering to stop and eat something solid. But I was too tired to eat, and too tired to argue with anyone, even my little voice.

I took a deep breath of the city into my nicotine stained lungs through the open window of the Lotus.

The warm night air of the Fraser Valley washed over me through the open car window offering to keep me awake. Most people think the smell of cauldron smog is revolting, but not I. To me it smells like ambrosia. I guess it was the big city guy bred into me by my late parents.

Maybe, rather than drive home, I should have taken up Liz's offer. Sure she was a hot dame, but I had rules concerning grateful clients. And rule number one: never sleep with a client. Sleeping with broads who pay your bills too often leads to avoidable and frequently messy complications.

It had taken me six days to cast Liz's personal demon into the hell it came from, and she was so grateful she offered me a sleep over.

I was amazed when she actually looked sad when I refused and instead accepted her healthy check. Five hundred a day plus expenses was the going rate; if I slept with every beautiful client I worked for I wouldn't feel right about taking their money. After all once in awhile even I need to eat, but man, did that doll have some gams…whew….

My oldest friend, Owlen Yonkers Vay, was my contact inside the Ye Olde Vancouver PD. He was the senior detective on the Y.O. Paranormal Investigative Service Squad—these days all companies use the Ye Olde tag at the beginning of their company name.

Russ Crossley

Owlen and I shorten the tag to Y.O. because it had made the Yellow Pages obsolete. And we loved the Yellow Pages--and my former college roommate.

Long before he worked for PISS, Owlen and I attended Y. O. Magic Arts College together. Owlen made more of himself with his degree than I ever did.

Of course, the Y. O. Mythical Creatures Equal Employment Act of 1984 had opened the doors for trolls like Owlen, and others of his ilk too often shunned by society. These days he had equal access to job opportunities like everyone else.

Owlen was one smart troll who had taken every advantage of the situation and consequently had advanced quickly within the YOVPD hierarchy.

Having a best friend who was a gumshoe, and someone capable of overlooking some of those little nuisance laws, like; 'you have no rights, scumbag' that impede criminal investigations, certainly helped him impress his superiors

Owlen and I had quite the partnership. He was the crime fighter, well I was up to my butt in dames and dough...yeah, right....I wish.

I'd only left him two hours ago and now this call. Frankly, I was worried.

This was the second card-carrying corporate sorcerer shelved in the last two weeks. Someone was peeved with the purveyors of the magical arts.

I arrived to find the glowing glass and steel twin towers of the Ye Olde Fortunate Message Corporation headquarters building protected by a phalanx of black and white police units.

After parking my car across the street from the artificial barrier of steel and flashing lights, I walked toward one of the uniforms keeping away non-existent crowds.

I didn't recognize the flatfoot outside. As you'd expect he looked bored stiff so I assumed he wasn't in the best of moods. I recognized the signs of donut deprivation in the poor guy, sleepy eyes, and a grim expression meant he must be low on sugar, fat, and caffeine.

Time to put my best foot forward. As I approached, I forced my lips into a wide smile and pulled out my identification.

Holding out my wallet, so he could clearly see my Ye Olde Licensed Investigator Association card, I said, "Rex Filagree, at the request of Detective Vay..."

The uniforms lackluster expression gave me a once over then he took the offered identification wallet from me. His grey eyes scanned the picture and my tombstone details. Without saying anything to me, he thumbed the radio mike clipped to his uniform shirt epaulette. "I gotta private dick here to see Vay..."

I heard Owlen's gruff voice come over the small speaker on the portable radio hanging off the uniforms black leather utility belt. "Let 'im through." The uniform grunted, stepped aside and handed me back my wallet.

I arrived at the executive penthouse to find Owlen's partner, Simone Langmack, standing leaning against the hallway wall with her arms crossed over her chest waiting for me. Her green eyes lit up and a grin crossed her tanned face when she saw me. I envied her shoulder length red curls that flowed off her wide shoulders.

Her hair always looked freshly quaffed no matter what time of day it was. She wore her usual ensemble of male-rapper-fit black slacks, two-sizes-too-large military style khaki shirt, and low heel boots, all designed to hide her figure from the casual observer.

The woman's body was one of the great mysteries of the twenty-first century. My dreams were too often filled with a longing to dig deeper into this woman's secrets.

Truth be told when Simi became Owlen's partner I'd thought about dating her, but then there was my rule number two: don't date a cop. They ask too many questions about your business.

I smiled warmly at her and tipped back my fedora with a flick of my index finger. "Hey, Simi, you're looking fantastic as usual…where's the big guy?"

Her eyes flashed and a crooked grin crossed her high cheek-boned face. "He's inside with the vic…" she nodded at the doorway over her right shoulder.

"You kno—"

Owlen's growl cut me off. "Hey, you two, stop jawin' out there. Either get a room and be done with it, or get your butts in here and help me find this guy some justice."

Simi shrugged and whispered to me, "Even for a troll he's in a nasty mood."

I offered her a tight, but understanding, smile and nodded. I went into the room first with her following behind me.

The conference room was a large, long room.

It extended at least a hundred and fifty feet or more along the side of the office tower. There was limited lighting. The only light in the room came from a series of pot lights recessed into the ceiling that ran parallel down either side of the long conference table in the middle of the room. One wall was comprised of smoked glass. Since it was still the middle of the night, the glass reflected the glow from the pot lights blocking the view outside.

No doubt in the daytime the windows offered a terrific view of the sprawling city of parks. The building faced west and was tall enough that you could see Stanley Park and the ocean from the bank of windows on a clear day.

As I said in the center of the room was a long solid onyx table with rows of black leather office chairs on either side of the table. The set up was such that sixty executives could be seated simultaneously in the conference room, which isn't surprising given the size of a corporation the likes of Y. O. Fortunate Message. They were after all the largest manufacturer of specialty messages inserted into fortune cookies worldwide.

The messages were in reality instant spells. There were spells for love, family, money, health, happiness, luck…whatever the user needed there was an instant spell for them.

Seated at end of the long table was a figure of a man dressed in a very expensive blue pinstripe suit laying face down in a large white bowl. Slowly I walked toward what I knew to be the recently deceased Vice-President of Sorcery until I stood looking down at the unmoving body.

The pale hands rested flat on either side of the bowl. I could very easily see the won-ton noodles floating around the head of dark hair like miniature pillows, though it was obvious this man hadn't died of natural causes. Not with the back of his skull caved in.

Once I was at the end of the table, I spotted Owlen standing next to the chair holding the body of dead executive. His wide mouth, filled with misshapen teeth, was busy mangling a stick of gum.

He quit smoking ten years ago. Since then he had the bouquet of ode de Juicy Fruit surrounding him 24/7. His red-rimmed eyes were peering into his notebook where his small, gnarled hands were busy scratching his notes.

Concentration furrowed his wide forehead. Without looking up he said, "Well, hotshot you've been here five minutes notice anything unusual?"

"Yup," I said. "No egg rolls."

∗∗∗

The next morning — after five hours sleep — Owlen sat across from me behind his scarred imitation pine office desk. The overhead fan swung lazily barely moving the stifling, mould-tinged air. Cheap wooden shades covered the windows that looked out over the parking lot of the Ye Olde Paranormal Investigative Service of the VPD.

Sitting beside me was, Maury Ping, CEO of Ye Olde Fortunate Message Corporation. He was a gray haired man who looked older than his fifty-five years. He was wringing his hands as if he were continually washing them, and he fidgeted in the low-backed pleather chair. His azure eyes were angry.

"I don't get it...how could someone murder Allan? It's impossible—"

"He's dead, Mr. Ping. That's all we know with certainty," said Owlen. His gum popped. It was audible even above the squeak of the fan over our heads. "I didn't say it was murder. What I said is the death is suspicious."

Obviously, Owlen hadn't told Ping that Allan Unnoté died of headbashedinitis. Smart guy, my buddy.

Ping shook his head and removed his wire-rimmed glasses. He pinched his nose between two fingers as if he was suffering from migraine headache number forty-seven, which maybe he was.

"This is impossible..." he murmured. "What am I going to tell the shareholders...we're finished..."

I glanced at Owlen his right eyebrow was arched and his fingers were steepled across his pudgy belly. His lifted his short legs, crossed them and plopped them down on top of his desk. His shoes were unpolished. He said he was trying for the Colombo look.

Said it caused suspects to drop their guard if they thought he was a lazy slob. And I thought he was just plain lazy.

Mr. Ping was right of course. If they didn't get a new sorcerer — an interchangeable term with wizard for those who prefer — within a few days, their competitors would cast spells that would quickly cause them to bankrupt. Corporate sorcerers cast protection spells and intense defense spells to protect companies from other sorcerers.

If one company was sorcererless for even a short time it created a sorcerer-gap that other corporations would quickly take advantage of.

That's the good old free market economy for you. Rival sorcerers would create such a twisting maze of spells that by the time a new sorcerer was hired it might take weeks or months to unravel the mess. By then it was always too late.

There were rumors that some sorcerers had set up worm or virus spells that would automatically activate when a sorcerer died or left a job suddenly. Everyone knew this practice, and fear of mutual-assured-bankruptcy kept everyone in line.

The system had become so complex, and the balance of magical energy so delicate, that any disruption in the mystical continuum could have devastating consequences.

In the previous murder case, two weeks ago, the Ye Olde Wing-of-Bat-Eye-of-Newt Compotation—they made the tin take out containers for Chinese food delivery, but not the cardboard lids—went bankrupt within two days of the murder. The resulting delivery-container-gap was so serious that governments had sent in military units to make emergency delivery containers. All involved knew this was temporary and that a permanent solution had to be found and soon.

Word on the street was that several smaller suppliers were considering joining forces.

As you would expect the key was whose sorcerer would be appointed Vice-President of Sorcery in the new, much larger company.

Obviously, these companies were first on our suspect list but so far we'd found no connection. If our list of suspect companies did not also produce instant spells for fortune cookies then this case worse than I first thought. It meant the culprit in both of these murders was unrelated to their competitors. If you eliminate greed as the killers motive that leaves crimes of passion, insurance scams, or the most dreaded enemy of crime…the megalomaniac!

"Mr. Ping." I leaned forward in my chair to peer at him. "I'm sympathetic to your loss, and I appreciate what this means to your company but, sir, we have a far larger problem…"

His confused eyes locked on mine. "Like what?" he said.

"We have an unknown maniac killing sorcerers, thus it seems reasonable to suggest someone has set into motion a plan to undermine the very pillars of our civilization."

To my surprise a withering smile crossed Ping's lips. He leaned back in his chair and crossed his arms over his sunken chest. His Armani suit rustled softly in the silence.

"Yeah. Right…" he laughed. "Aren't we being a bit melodramatic, detective? I've been in this business a long time, and I've seen a lot of strange things. There was the time the Ye Olde Catch-Me-If-You-Can Corporation's wizard unleashed the Dragon of Akron. They cornered the paper plate market after that little ploy. And then there was the Ye Olde Saucy-Sexy-Spicy Corporation, and their attempt to kidnap their competitors junior sorcerer and hold her for ransom, then —"

"There is a big difference between those friendly little competitor pranks, and murder, Mr. Ping," interrupted Owlen. "Murder is my business…"

Ping shot Owlen a look of distain. "What would a troll know about competition?"

Such prejudicial statements weren't anything new to either of us, but this case was different. The stakes were higher and it seemed to me Ping was deliberately being confrontational. It was as if he were trying to get a rise out of us, particularly Owlen.

Owlen dropped his feet off his desk and glared at Ping. I knew he was only acting the offended party. I had seen him do this before. In reality, Owlen is the gentlest troll I have ever known.

"Mr. Ping, I suggest you keep your decorum within the limits of my tolerance while I attempt to get to the bottom of the murder of Allan Unnoté. Don't you wish me to catch the culprit?"

Ping sagged against his chair back and sighed heavily. He was like a beaten man looking into an abyss from which there is no return. "Of course, detective…I'm sorry…it's just that —"

Owlen smiled. "That's okay, Mr. Ping, you're forgiven. Now please tell us everything you know about Mr. Allan Unnoté."

***

Our interview with Ping yielded fresh fruit. We were now in the Chinese food supply district looking for the small supply company, whose name Ping gave us, where legend had it Unnoté first came to the notice of a corporate head hunter.

Ping told us Unnoté was single, forty-five, and held a Class A Wizard Certification from the Y.O. Magical Arts Bar Association.

The question raised by these facts, for Owlen and me, was how did a class A come to be socerering for such a low-level supply company? The size of this supply company was indicative of low paying sweatshops staffed by illegal immigrants. Perhaps Unnoté was an illegal?

Before we checked him out with the immigration authorities, we thought we better first check with his previous employer.

When we walked through the front door of the Ye Olde Pork Fat Palace, I thought for a second I had stepped through a time warp.

The place reeked of incense and rendered fat and there was a haze of greasy smoke. Unfortunately, the incense did not mask the heavy, slick feel of the place. That's about the only way I can describe the feeling of the room on the exposed skin of my hands and face.

Against one wall was a row of wooden stave barrels containing what appeared to be substances of dubious origin. The ancient walls were thick with age and stained with decades of cooking fat and the walls themselves looked to be comprised of boards peeling with age, barely able to support the sagging roof. I expected the whole kit-and-caboodle to collapse on our heads at any moment.

The owner, Mr. Benson Stein — I recognized him from the wall of employee of the month pictures behind the cash register — approached us with a wide smile in his weathered features. His gray hair was receding and would soon retreat completely. He was slim and stood no more than five foot six inches tall.

His calloused hand grasped mine as we greeted each. His grip was firm, in fact too firm. I winced behind my smile as he pumped my hand vigorously. Owlen grunted as Stein took one of his gnarled hands in his and did the same.

"How can I help you, gentlemen?"

I was relieved Stein wanted to get down to business. Skip the small talk. Good.

Owlen flipped open his badge wallet to reveal his gold shield. Stein nodded, his eyes knowing. "Yes, detective, I knew you were cops when you walked through my front door."

I wasn't surprised. Stein had been in this neighborhood for many years and probably knew everyone's coming and goings. Two strangers with paper-pusher-office hands certainly weren't locals, and we didn't dress well enough for executives or lawyers. Owlen was a little short for a health inspector. And since I was dressed in a tan raincoat and fedora, we couldn't be anything but cops, or crooks.

We hadn't stuck a gun in his face, as soon when we walked in, and didn't say things like youse guys, so we weren't mobsters. This left pretty much cops. I resisted the urge to call the guy Sherlock freakin' Holmes to his face.

Owlen pulled out a picture of the late Allan Unnoté that he'd downloaded off the company's website. "We have information this man used to work for you?"

Stein took the picture and gazed at it for several seconds. "Yeah. But that was a long time ago…and…"

"What's wrong?" I noted the puzzled expression on Stein's face.

Stein frowned and flipped the picture over. The back was blank. "What's this man's name?"

"Unnoté, Allan Unnoté," said Owlen. "Why?"

"Well, that explains it…this isn't the man that worked for me." Stein handed the picture back to Owlen who threw me a surprised glance.

"But, sir we have information that he was recruited for the position of Vice-President of Sorcery for the Ye Olde Fortunate Message Corporation from your company—" I explained

Stein shook his head. "No. Can't be. If it is him then he looked very different, and if you know him as Unnoté then it definitely can't be the man that worked for me. His name was Kulpepper, Mark Kulpepper. And he was a sorcerer Class C. Fortunate Message would never hire a Class C for a Class A position. I mean that would be stupid." Stein shrugged. "The head hunter would have to be an idiot or…"

"What is it, Mr. Stein?" I asked. I could clearly see the wheels turning behind those black eyes.

"Well...there is another possibility..." He shook his head as if discarding the idea. "Naw. Besides it's only a rumor..."

Owlen grunted. "Rumor or not please enlighten me, Mr. Stein."

Stein considered Owlen's words. "Okay, but please don't laugh."

I crossed my heart. "I swear, and he..." indicating Owlen, "lost his sense of humor last week." Owlen winced at my lame joke.

Stein didn't seem to notice. He lowered his voice as he spoke. "There's a rumor about a mob boss recruiting Class C Wizards who are provided false documents that show they're Class A Wizards. When the corporate headhunters show up they think they've stumbled upon a real find. Reputations are made. Copious amounts of money change hands. And everyone is happy. But word on the street is in exchange for career advancement the class C's pass on corporate secrets to the mob."

Owlen looked at me and I looked at him. "No. Reaaaaally," I said.

Stein shrugged. His weathered face bore a look of disgust and he threw his hands skyward in mock surrender. "See! I knew you wouldn't believe me. After all I'm just some ignorant pork fat salesman. What do I know?"

He was about to walk away in a huff when Owlen stopped him. "Just a moment, Mr. Stein. I believe you." Owlen must have seen the surprised look on my face because I opened my mouth to speak and he cast me a look that told me I had better keep my mouth shut.

"What's this mob boss's name?"

"Huh...I was told never to say his name out loud..."

Owlen handed Stein his notebook and pen, the page was blank. "Here, write it down."

Stein took the pen and the notebook and wrote down the name. Just as he printed the last letter all hell broke loose.

***

My head was pounding like I had been on a week long bender when I woke up on the stretcher in the back of the ambulance. A dusky skinned woman with a stethoscope round her neck, and a small, sad smile on her lips, looked down on me.

"Can you understand me, Mr. Filagree?" she said.

"Huh…yeah…what happened?"

"I'm told a sneaker bomb materialized inside the former Mr. Stein's pork fat shop, and exploded…"

I raised my head too quickly and black spots danced before my eyes. I lay my head back down and groaned.

She smiled weakly. "Don't worry. You'll be fine in a few days. Good thing for you Mr. Stein was standing in front of you when the bomb exploded or you'd all be dead…"

Owlen…where was Owlen? "What about Detective Vay?"

She shook her head slowly and her dark eyes avoided me. "I'm sorry…"

My oldest friend was dead, and with him our only lead.

And I was so quick to dismiss the rumor. I wanted to curl up and die right there. But first I had to find Owlen's killer. And I knew who the chief suspect was. The mob boss, whoever he was, was going to pay.…

And I knew who was going to help me get him…Simi…

***

As I expected, Simi was already on the scene of the burned and blackened pork fat shop working with the bomb squad and forensic technicians to sift the wreckage for evidence of the bomb making materials.

I walked purposefully up to the grim faced redhead who was so engrossed in her conversation with one of the techs that at first she didn't notice me. Sensing my presence she cut off her words and her watery eyes locked on mine.

Suddenly she wrapped her arms around me and pressed herself to me. I wrapped my arms around her. We didn't exchange any words for several seconds holding on to each as if we'd never let go. Finally, we released each other.

Stepping back, I saw the tears in her eyes. "I…" The words caught in my throat.

She placed one finger on my lips. "It's okay, Rex, we don't need to talk about this right now. We'll deal with it later."

A sense of relief washed over me. "You're right, of course, Simi."

She pulled out Owlen's notebook. It was tinged black and curled at the edges, but in the middle of the page there was written two words: The Pixie.

"Pixie? Pixie's are small winged sprites. They're friendly little creatures not mob bosses," I said.

Simi shook her head and pointed to the word 'the'. "Not a pixie, the…" she said, careful not to say the mob bosses full name. Good thing too, we didn't need another sneaker bomb going off.

"What do you know about this, pixie?"

"Plenty. Owlen has been hot on the trail of this mob boss for five years."

"He never said anything to me."

She chuckled. "You tell jokes, boyo…"

Owlen. Why did he leave me out of this investigation? Were the stakes too high? Was the risk too high? Any way you cut it, Simi and I were going to find this pixie and rip his wings off.

"Ok, where do we find this pixie?"

"A new lead came in shortly after last night's murder. I expect he was going to follow it up after you two left Steins. I think it was going to be his next sto—" Her voice cracked with emotion and tears welled up in her red- rimmed eyes. I rested one hand on her shoulder and nodded.

"It's ok," I said softly. "Let me see the lead." Simi nodded and flipped to another the charred page of Owlen's notebook.

An address. 'No. 9 Street of Dreams'.

***

We arrived on the Street of Dreams to find a faux oak door set in the heritage redbrick building that displaying a wrought iron No. 9. I was surprised it was a muffin and coffee shop called Y. O. Bubble-Bubble-Toil-And-Muffins.

Curious. I thought mob bosses usually worked from bars, strip clubs, or other similar seedy establishments. Mobsters and muffins... who would have thought?

When we went inside our senses were assaulted by the smell of fresh baked muffins and coffee. My stomach growled like a Persian pussycat in heat and I realized I hadn't eaten today and very little yesterday. All I'd eaten these past twenty-four hours was a couple of egg rolls from a drive through place after Owlen and I left Fortunate message.

"Mind if I get something?" I said.

Simi shook her head while her green eyes scanned the shop. A large swarthy man wearing a loose fitting pale yellow golf shirt — with a Y.O. New Community Golf Course logo over the breast pocket — stood behind the counter reading a magazine. When we walked in the large man hadn't bothered to glance up to see who had entered. His bulging biceps told me this was not a man to be taken lightly.

To his right was a glass case behind which was a selection of muffins. There was acorn and apple, batwing-blueberry, sinful-strawberry, bubble-bubble-bran, and a wide variety of eclectic combinations like, dragon egg and oatmeal, and toe of lizard and lemon. That last one was too much for my low blood sugar.

My stomach twisted at the thought of the dreadful mix of flavors from some of these concoctions so I decided to go au-natural.

"Hi," I said brightly as I approached the counter. The mob guy looked over his magazine and sighed. He slapped the magazine down on the counter a withering look on his face.

"I'd like a blueberry, please."

He stood unmoving staring at me his dark eyes unflinching. Under his steady gaze, I felt the trickle of a single bead of sweat run down my back.

"It's ok, Sonny," said a high-pitched voice coming from floor-length gold curtain behind the mob guy whose name was apparently Sonny. "Give da guy his muffin."

Sonny grunted walked to the case and picked a blueberry off the plate of three. He snapped a plain white paper bag open and dropped the muffin into it. He wrapped his meaty fingers around the bag and squashed the muffin into a small ball then placed it on the counter.

"That'll be three bucks," said Sonny.

There was a bone-chilling cackle from behind the curtain.

A six-foot tall, pixie who had to top out easily at four hundred pounds walked through the curtain.

I studied this pixie with his royal purple curls of wispy hair on his head, and pointed ears, and thin gossamer wings sticking above his wide shoulders. The angry scar running down the right side of his face, his swollen lips, and beady eyes gave me the shivers. He was the ugliest pixie I had ever seen.

He was dressed in black slacks, and a white sleeveless undershirt. A long smoldering cigar was between his blood-red lips.

"Are you — ?"

"Don't say it," said Sonny his eyes warning me.

I nodded.

"Yup, it's him," said Simi behind me.

The obese pixie's eyes narrowed giving him a truly evil appearance. "Who're youse guys?"

"Cops —" grunted Sonny.

The pixie slapped Sonny hard across the back of his meaty head and the henchman fell to the shop floor with a loud bang.

"I didn't ask you!"

"Huh…my name's Filagree. This is Detective Langmack."

A wicked smile crossed The Pixies ugly features. "I know youse… Rex Filagree…right?"

"Huh…yeah…"

"What do ya want with me?"

I felt several more lines of perspiration roll down my back. "My friend Owlen Vay was killed earlier today and we were told you might be involved…"

The Pixie grinned. His large right hand pushed the crushed muffin toward me. "Tell you what, Filagree, why don't you take the muffin on the house and get outta here before I get real angry with ya. Ok? I'd hate to see you get hurt." He winked at me.

The anger, grief, and the pure rage surfaced in me about the brutal murder of my best friend. I turned and faced Simi. She took one look at me and saw the rage in me about to explode.

Her eyes went wide as I bolted toward her and tackled her as if she were a running back carrying both of us toward the front door.

The door slammed aside with a bang. We fell to the floor and rolled toward the open door. Simi's head hit the floor hard and I saw her eyes glaze over.

"The Pixie!" I said as we went out the door. I pressed my body over hers to protect her as the bomb suddenly appeared and immediately exploded.

Shredded bits of flaming muffin shop buried us. I felt the heat of flames on my back. It took me several seconds to regain my bearings as I was still disoriented from the force of the blast.

Finally, with my lungs seemingly on fire, I rolled off Simi, slipped my burning tan raincoat off my shoulders, and kicked it away from us.

I slipped my arms underneath Simi, picked her up, and carried her away from the intense heat, smoke, and the crackling orange, red, and blue flames.

I finally collapsed to the pavement in the middle of Street of Dreams coughing and staring back at the wreckage of the Pixie's muffin shop. I was certain no one could survive that inferno.

Simi moaned. I looked at her, slipped one hand under her head, and lifted her up. Her eyes fluttered open.

"What happened?" she said.

"The Pixie's out of business."

Her eyes went wide. "What did you do?"

A smiled weakly. "I took him out."

"Owww...my head hurts," she said.

I heard the sound of a siren. The medics would be here soon. "I know. And I'm sorry."

She smiled softly. "Its okay, Rex."

I laughed. "Ya know, Simi, I may just have broken one of my rules."

She looked at me her brow furrowed.

I laughed again. "It's ok. I'll explain later. Right now why don't we enjoy the fire."

She relaxed and looked at me with a sloppy grin on her beautiful face, her green eyes sparkling with mirth.

We sat in silenced waiting for the help that would soon arrive.

Owlen was dead. The Pixie was dead. But Simi and I were alive. And we would be responsible to carry on what Owlen started. Justice had been served.

I reached into the pocket of my pants and pulled out the baggie I had been saving. I threw it toward the dancing heat of the fire. It landed next to the flames and was quickly smoldering. Soon the plastic would melt and the contents would be consumed.

"What was that?" said Simi.

"Egg rolls."

"Why?"

I shrugged. "With death you get the egg roll."

Simi nodded. "Yeah. Egg rolls. Too bad Owlen never got his."

"Yeah. Too bad."

One Red Shoe

OPERATIVE MADDIE SUREFOOT STUDIED THE SHOE. It was sure a big one, at least twenty feet high. She'd never seen one like it before. It looked familiar but she didn't know where she'd seen it before. All she knew for sure was she had seen this shoe before.

Reaching inside her cotton suit jacket she pulled out her cell phone from her inside pocket and pressed the quick dial number for her section chief.

Barb Wallup's voice answered after one buzz at the other end.

"Maddie. What's up?" She sounded impatient. The boss must be having a bad day.

Maddie had already considered the summary of what she'd seen in her mind before she made the call. "Hi, Barb, I'm at the scene now and it's exactly as reported by eyewitnesses."

Barb snorted. "I thought I'd seen everything." The chief paused. Maddie knew what was coming. "Any idea how it got there?"

The million-dollar question. She had considered all possibilities, but nothing she'd thought of made sense expect one, and she didn't want to think about that. "No. There doesn't appear to be any reasonable explanation. So far."

"How about unreasonable explanations?"

"If you mean do I have a theory then, yes I might have one."

There was silence on the other end of the line. A pause that spoke volumes. Barb Wallup was a practical woman who liked her explanations clean and simple. The Internal Secrets Bureau collected and hid many strange things from the general public, but everything had a rational explanation as far as Barb was concerned, no matter how fantastic.

"Ok, Maddie, try me."

Maddie sucked in a breath then let it out slowly. "I think this is the home of the woman who lived in a shoe, who had so many children she didn't know what to do."

There was a long pause. So long in fact, Maddie began to think Barb had hung up. Finally her chief asked, "You know what this means don't you?"

Maddie swallowed hard as her heart rate increased finally she said, "Yes. It means the giant is back in town."

***

Rednose the giant hadn't been seen in fifty years. If this was his shoe it meant he and his wife Brunhilda had been fighting again and the shoe had been tossed out of his kingdom on the other side of reality.

The land of unreality was the realm where there were giants, elf's, unicorns, and goblins, wizards and witches, and other creatures too terrible to dream of. The barrier between reality and unreality hadn't been breached since the beanstalk was cut down five decades ago.

Before she married her father, Maddie's mother, Irish McComb, had been an ISB operative. Irish had chopped down the beanstalk in time to stop the invasion of reality by unreality.

These days it would be simple if all the ISB had to deal with were vampires, alien invaders, or giant mutant insects, but an invasion from unreality? That was every ISB operative's worst nightmare.

Maddie's mother had saved reality barely in the nick of time, this time her daughter might not be so lucky. Too bad the cameras in those days were the size of a terrier and her mother had dropped hers while trying to climb down the beanstalk so fast or they'd have pictures of the giant and his castle. A lay of the land would be very useful of they were going to plan an adequate defense.

If the chief had her way they'd be planning a full scale preemptive assault rather than defense, but Maddie convinced Barb there was a better way than war.

Maddie stood on the cement walkway looking up to the porch that ran along the Victorian style house that was known to the world as the Shade Tree Seniors Residence. (STSR is the cover name for the Retired Spies, Saboteurs, and Terrorists Rest Home and Bingo Emporium. Apparently retired spies, saboteurs, and terrorists love to play bingo. Who knew?)

Maddie clipped the alligator clip attached to the top edge of her ISB identification badge to the breast pocket of her suit jacket. She took a deep breath then released it. She hadn't visited her mother for two months, so she'd have to listen to complaints about what a bad daughter she was. She could hear her mother saying that just because Maddie was off on dangerous secret missions, facing death at every turn didn't mean she couldn't find time to visit her elderly mother.

Since every internal organ in her mother's body had been replaced, and she'd been genetically enhanced in every way known to medical science, Maddie's mother was far from elderly. But nevertheless Maddie'd hear about her less than exemplary offspring skills.

She arrived at the front door of what looked to passersby as just another ordinary house on an ordinary street in an ordinary small town in America.

What the world didn't know was behind this door was the most modern facility yet built to house the retired veterans of the secret wars of the past eighty years.

The door had no doorknob and there was no mailbox. The windows old-fashioned wood framed windows on either side of door reflected the street and the yard but they were like one-way mirrors. Whoever was on the other side could see out, but Maddie couldn't see what was on the other side.

Not that it mattered. She knew what was inside. She'd been here often enough. Just not lately, she thought.

Maddie reached inside her suit jacket and took out her id wallet. She took out the proxima card she kept there and ran it over a section of wall next to the door.

There was a barely audible click and the door slide aside into the doorframe. Mattie waited until the familiar mechanical voice spoke.

"Identify," it said. She'd never been able to determine if the voice was male or female not that it mattered, but intellectual games were something she enjoyed.

"Madeline Surefoot. Operative number 27, Internal Secrets Bureau."

There was a two second delay (yes, Maddie counted the elapsed time) then the voice said, "Identity verified. You may enter."

"Thank you." Though it was unnecessary to thank a machine Maddie had always considered politeness a worthwhile human virtue that separated them from the machines, and the beings in unreality that she considered non-human.

After she stepped through the open door it slide closed with a whoosh and a soft thud. Before her was the reception area with it's waterfall in one corner of the wide, carpeted lobby.

The waterfall fell into an oval shaped pond bordered by a small forest of dwarf palm tress and tropical ferns and flowering pants. The variety and splash of color and the bubble of water striking the small pond had always given Maddie a sense of inner peace.

She cringed inside when she saw Rocky Almost was working reception today. He was obviously on the telephone, speaking into his headset, his gray eyes focused on the flat screen monitor in front of him.

She and Rocky had dated for six months, until she discovered he had been living with another woman for over a year even after they began to date. She'd forgiven him, but it still hurt her to her core to see him. Ever since Rocky her trust of the male gender had never been at such a low level as it was now.

She approached the desk just as he ended the call. "Thanks and have a nice day." Rocky pressed a finger against the side of the headset.

Her mouth formed a tight smile as she tried to catch his attention. "Hi, Rocky," she said brightly.

He looked up from his monitor at her but he didn't smile. "Hello, Ms. Surefoot."

The use of her last name hurt Maggie worse than if he'd called her every four-letter word in the dictionary. Whatever they had once felt for each was truly dead and gone. It was like they'd never know each other at all.

"I'm here to see my mother," she said, letting the smile fall away from her lips.

"Ok." He glanced at her id badge then placed a clipboard with an excel spreadsheet-style form and a pen attached by a string. There were columns for names, dates and times. He pointed with his index finger to the next empty space on the form. "Name date and time," he said, his tone dull.

"I know the drill," she said, restraining herself from snapping the words out. Given his hard exterior it seemed unlikely he'd be affected in the least anyway.

She completed the form then turned and walked away headed for the corridor than ran down the middle of the first floor. Behind her she heard him say, "Have a nice visit."

Maddie hesitated then rushed away, the knuckles of her right hand white from gripping the strap of her handbag that hung off her right shoulder.

She held back tears and her heart beat hard in her chest. She suppressed her emotions as she hurried down then wide tiled hallway past the recreation room, the theater and the gymnasium. Along the way she met several residents she knew.

Mrs. Campbell, a retired MI6 agent, Mr. Nahan, retired from Kenya's National Security Intelligence Service, and Mr. Yamanta, from Japan's Giant Monster Intelligence Bureau. She nodded at each one as she passed them. Mr. Yamanta had been living here for more than sixty years, but he didn't look a day over sixty himself. Maddie wish she knew the secret to his longevity.

Finally she arrived at her mother's room. She closed her eyes took a deep breath then released it slowly. After wiping her cheeks with the back of her hand she opened her eyes and rapped her knuckles on the door.

"Come in, dahlin," she heard her mother's distinctive southern accent come through the door.

Maddie pasted a smile on her face then opened the door. "Hi, Mom."

She froze when she realized her mother wasn't alone. A very elegant man stood next to her cream-colored chaise lounger.

He had a perfectly trimmed goatee that formed a sharp point on the end of his angular chin. Stuck in one eye socket was a monocle, and he wore a black velvet smoking jacket and perfectly pressed gray slacks. A fire engine red scarf surrounded his thin neck. It was tucked down the front of his jacket.

Her mother looked the same as always. Her dyed black hair was piled atop her head perfectly permed into tight curls. Upon seeing her daughter she leapt to her feet seeming to fly off the lounger, and threw her arms wide and ran at Maddie and wrapped her arms around her and hugged her tightly. Maddie thought about drawing her weapon.

"Maddie! My dahlin girl! How long has it been?"

It had been what ten seconds and her mother had already started berating her for not visiting. "Two months, Mom. I'm sorry, I—"

Her mother startled her when she laughed brightly and released her. Her mother's eyes were bright and cheerful and she wore a wide smile on her face. Most importantly her eyes reflected her happiness.

Had her mother been smoking wacky-tabaccy, or was she drunk?

One of Maddie's eyebrows arched. There wasn't the telltale smell of marijuana smoke and she hadn't detected liquor on her mother's breath when she hugged her.

Hugged me? Maybe her mother had been assimilated by aliens? It had been known to happen. "Mom? Are you okay?"

It was then she realized her mother was dressed in a beautiful silk kimono that flowed around her body giving her the illusion of floating on air. Her mother laughed again then went to sprawl once again on the chaise lounger again. "No, no, dahlin', I'm fine. I'm just in love is all." Her mother waved a hand at her. "Silly girl. Haven't you ever been in love?"

Maddie knew love, but she'd never seen her mother in love. Her father had disappeared when she was a little girl.

Seeing her mother this way was a new and strange experience.

"Yeah, Mom, of course, but you haven't..." Maddie hesitated, as her face grew warm. "You haven't been in love as long as..." Her voice trailed off. Had her mother loved her father? She had no idea; it wasn't something they'd ever talked about.

"Yes, muh dear daughter. I loved your father very much, but he's not coming back from the fourth dimension." She paused to grin at Maddie. "I'd like you to meet Lord Blacktoe, my fiancée."

The elegant looking man who'd bee silently observing them turned toward Maddie and held out one hand. "Charmed, Ms. Surefoot."

Maddie took his hand in hers and cringed inside. It was like shaking the tail of a dead fish. "Pleased to meet you, Lord Blacktoe, so you wish to marry my mother?"

"Yes, Ms. Surefoot, I'm madly in love." Was he kidding? It was like he'd just told her he preferred marmalade on his toast.

Maddie offered him a tight smile then turned toward her mother. "Mother, I'm afraid I'm not here for a social call. There has been some trouble I need to talk to you about." She indicated Lord Blacktoe with a slight nod. "In private."

"Oh, poo, poo, dahlin', Alfie is MI6. Retired, o' course. He's cleared to the highest level. Something' he calls the Official Secrets Act says if he tells anyone the Brits have to kill him. I'm shore he won't tell anyone. " Her mother batted her eyes at Lord Blacktoe. "Isn't that right, Alfie?"

The man's expression remained stoic he nodded his head ever so slightly, after his eyes had flitted between them. Did his expression ever change even when he was...Maddie pushed away the unimaginable image before it took hold in her mind. She shuddered and wanted to roll her eyes but managed not stop herself.

"Sure, Mom, no problem. Anyway, we found this big red shoe and—"

"The giant," her mother interrupted her. As if she were a balloon she sagged into the cushions of the lounger and her features went slack as all color drained from her cheeks. "He's back," she whispered.

Maddie crossed her arms over her chest. "That's what we thought, until intelligence confirmed the bridge to unreality was still closed. There have been no other intrusions. At least that we know of."

Her mother's smooth forehead wrinkled. Sometimes Maddie thought with all the surgery her mother was starting to look younger than she did. "Then it has to be Jack," said her mother.

"Who?" Maddie's heart rate increased.

Her mother looked into her eyes, her features were taunt and her eyes seemed to bore into her daughters. "Jack, dear. Of Jack and the Beanstalk."

***

Maddie steered her Aston Martin DB9 into an empty parking stall that surrounded Beanstalk Park. The site where the beanstalk had been chopped down over fifty years ago was now a national monument surrounded by a park complete with picnic tables, a children's playground, and barbecue pits. It was a favorite spot for weekend family outings.

Since today was Saturday there were a myriad of Volvo station wagons and minivans occupying every other parking stall in the lot. Maddie's tricked out sports car was going to stick out like a frog in an onion field.

Maddie turned off the engine and got out. She kept her dark sunglasses on as she strolled toward the thirty-yard wide stump. The stump was all that remained of the once awe-inspiring beanstalk that ended in unreality.

There was a sign between two steel posts embedded deep into the grass in front of the stump. The sign gave a short history of the stump and the beanstalk, leaving out the important secret details of how it had been cut down and who had done the task.

Maddie's mother had used a laser gun to cut the stalk down. Fortunately the area where the great stalk had fallen had been mostly uninhabited so no one was hurt when it crashed to Earth. A few cows, some sheep, and a few rabbits, had been crushed, and seismographs around the world had registered six points on the Richter scale, but the property damage had been minimal. The ISB had paid off anyone who submitted a claim, a fact even Congress didn't know about. Black ops money was way off the books, and an operation like that cost huge amounts of cash.

Maddie sauntered up to the fence guarded the stump so the children wouldn't climb it and to prevent teenagers from carving their initials into the green stalk. Kids. Maddie shook her head and smiled to herself.

Her mother explained that the Jack who'd managed to transport the red shoe wasn't the original Jack. Apparently original Jack had been a very busy boy in unreality.

He had dated most of the female children of the old-woman-who-lived-in-a-shoe-who-had-so-many-children-she-didn't-know-what-to-do and the giant. She and the giant had sired several hundred children.

Before he left unreality, Jack, had fathered a lot of children. Apparently, the male children were all named Jack Junior. As stupid as it sounded it made sense when you had so many children you didn't know what to name them.

Maddie scanned the park from where she stood by the fence. Children, dogs, mom's and dad's, everyone enjoying the sunny warm weather. Maddie had to push away the sadness that gripped her. Her family had never enjoyed simple pleasures like a day the park. Her family had too often been apart separated by continents or dimensions or where ever the latest secret mission took them.

She'd never had any intention but to join the family business when she was old enough. Her mother once explained that being a spy was in the blood. Secret agent work was a family tradition going to back to the days when an Italian ancestor worked uncover as a Roman agent. Maximus Gallus Surefoot accompanied the Hannibal expedition. He sabotaged Hannibal's plans to conquer the Roman Empire.

Maddie frowned as her eyes settled on a man across the park. Near a stand of pine trees. He looked out of place. He was short, in fact so short; she suspected he was a little person (she decided she wouldn't mention it). He wore a black and white pinstriped suit and on his head he wore a straw hat titled to one side at a cocky angle. Most notably he was alone, like her.

She wondered what he was doing here in the park. Dark sunglasses covered his eyes and he appeared to be studying her. The most direct approach seemed the most practical.

She approached the little man her eyes warily flitting side-to-side looking for threats. The man didn't move. She continued when there were no obvious threats.

"Hello," she said as she came up to him.

"Hello, Operative 27." His voice had a surprisingly deep baritone quality to it.

Her eyes narrowed. "Do I know you?"

The corners of his curled. "No. But Chief Wallup does. She sent me."

Maddie's stomach muscles tightened. Obviously Barb didn't want to tell her about this contact. "Oh? Who are you then?"

"I'm with R&D." He paused, turned around and started to walk into the trees. "Follow me. I have something to show you."

Maddie hesitated. Walking into an unknown forest with a man she didn't know was reckless if not irresponsible. As a precaution Maddie reached into her suit jacket and pulled out her ASP semi-automatic pistol. She didn't want to shoot anyone but she would if cornered. The ASP was a good weapon for close quarters like this forest of trees.

The little man was quick so she was breathing hard when she arrived in the clearing. What she saw made her breath catch in her throat and she froze where she stood.

A two-story balloon floated above the mashed down grass in the clearing. It was tethered to the ground by ropes tied to wooden stakes pounded into the ground. Red, yellow and blue stripes covered the balloon.

The air was thick with the smell of rotting leaves and cut grass.

"Operative 27, come over here."

Maddie took in a breath and looked in the direction of the man's voice. Beside the balloon stood the man. He'd doffed his sunglasses revealing sapphire blue eyes.

"What's the balloon for?" Maddie asked as she holstered her gun beneath her jacket.

"I'm going to take you to unreality in this balloon." Maddie looked at him the surprise registering on her face. The man held out a business card.

Maddie took it and read his name was Mike Oz, PhD, Mac, Eng. "So you're the Wizard of Oz?" Maddie smirked. "Nice try, pal."

The little man laughed. "No, of course not. I'm a scientist and I'm going to take you to unreality in this balloon."

Maddie eyed Dr. Oz with one eyebrow cocked. She'd seen a lot of strange things; a balloon that would take her to unreality wasn't outside the realm of possibility.

"I thought the portal between reality and unreality wasn't accessible."

Dr. Oz shrugged. "It isn't, for most people."

"Do you have a permit?" Permits were required to travel to unreality. Maddie had never seen one but she knew it was a requirement.

"Uhhh…not exactly."

"Not exactly, huh? That's what I thought." Maddie turned to walk away. "I'm so outta here."

"Hold on, Ms. Surefoot." Maddie stopped. "Chief Wallup wants you to go. That's why she sent me to see you. It's dangerous, against the rules, and filled with adventure. Most importantly if we do this its very likely we'll save the world."

Maddie spun around a wide smile pasted to her tanned features.

"Now that's my kind of mission. Let's get this balloon in the air."

***

After three hours of flying time they arrived in unreality. The balloon floated on the warm air. Giant birds, with what looked like forty-foot wingspans, floated along side them their wings spread in order to ride the updrafts.

Maddie spotted the giant's castle first on the horizon the twin stone towers piercing the puffy white clouds. The same birds that now floated in the air around them had constructed nests along the castle walls and some sections of wall had collapsed reminiscent of a child that had lost baby teeth sporadically.

Had something happened to the giant?

They soon arrived at the castle and Dr. Oz managed to find a safe place to land amongst the stones that fell and landed haphazardly along the base of the castle walls. The castle and the surrounding area looked deserted.

The forest had encroached the park-like area that bordered the castle land, and the grass had grown waist high in sections.

What bothered Maddie was evidence of a battle. Large sections of grass had been burned black and some trees in the nearby forest were charred, some having collapsed, or the tree trunks were shattered before they were blown apart.

Who in unreality had the nerve and the firepower to go up against the giant?

What she didn't realize was the grounds were imbedded with sensors and their arrival had been noted.

Half an hour later a green army jeep broke from the forest. Three men rode in the vehicle with one man standing in the bed of the jeep manning a machine gun. Maddie watched their approach with trepidation. Whose army were these guys with?

All of the men wore reflective aviator glasses and the passenger had an unlit cigar between his teeth. The men's rippling biceps were bare, tanned and covered in scars.

The passenger had the butt of an automatic rifle resting on his thigh the barrel pointed to the sky.

"Hey, there, little lady," said the passenger over the squeal of the jeeps brakes as it stopped in front of them.

Maddie crossed her arms over her chest and shifted her weight to her left leg. "Name's ISB Operative Madeline Surefoot, not little lady." She reached into her pocket and pulled out her identification wallet and flashed her credentials.

The man chuckled and removed his sunglasses to reveal a warm brown eyes a woman could get lost in. "Sorry, Ms. Surefoot, name's Jack. I'm in charge of this military zone."

Maddie arched an eyebrow. "Really? You're Jack? Well, then, Jack, tell me what's happened here."

The smile dissipated from Jack's rugged features. "War. Death. Blood."

"Sorry? War? With whom?"

Jack got out of the jeep. Maddie was impressed. He was over six feet tall with a wide chest and muscular arms. He moved with the confidence and strength of someone who could handle himself. He threw the cigar to the ground then crushed it under his boot heel. "You've heard of the old woman who —"

"Yes. I know who she is. What about her?" Maddie was growing impatient. Barb wanted her in unreality for a reason, and it wasn't to play footsie with some soldier boy, as appealing as that might be. Jack was clearly handsome and just the type that would break her heart.

The guy probably had hot and cold running blondes back at base camp.

Jack eyed her with a sly grin on his lips. "My grandmother is leading the defense of unreality."

"Revolution? Against what? Fairy's and goblins?"

"Not exactly. You see —" The stone wall behind them exploded raining them with bits of rock and mortar. Smoke and dust filled Maddie's nose and mouth

"Com'on!" yelled Jack. "We have to go."

He jumped into the jeep while the man with the machine gun began firing sporadically into the forest. Maddie ran to the jeep with Dr. Oz close behind her.

Jack motioned for her to sit in his lap and Dr. Oz to climb into the back. Maddie considered protesting but another explosion to her right made up her mind. She sat across his lap and he wrapped one arm around her waist to keep from falling as the jeep jerked and started to drive in a zigzag pattern across the open parkland. Maddie locked her arms around Jack's neck and held on as the jeep swayed side to side and bounced across the open field.

The driver's features were grim and his arms were stiff with tension as he struggled to keep the jeep from rolling over due to the sudden increase in weight.

An explosion near the front left bumper sprayed them with dirt. The driver made a sharp turn to the right to avoid the crater created by whatever ordinance the enemy was using. Maddie felt like she'd lose her lunch. She tasted bile at the back of her throat.

The driver drove like a man possessed (which is entirely possible in unreality) until they rounded a cliff. With a wall between them the explosions stopped but the driver kept zigzagging.

After twenty minutes they arrived an encampment surrounded by guard towers on the four corners. Teams of men and women stood in the guard towers scanning the plains that ran away toward the granite cliff they'd left behind them. The jeep pulled up to a guardhouse and gate and came to a stop, the brakes squeaking loudly.

"Sergeant Jack Bean, Recon Unit 6." He indicated Maddie with a nod. "This is ISB Operative Surefoot. The guy in the back is Dr. Oz, ISB R&D."

The guard nodded. "Thank you, Sergeant. You may pass."

Maddie started when she heard the familiar sound of a bolt being cocked on a fifty caliber machine from somewhere above them.

She glanced at Jack. He offered a twisted smile. "The war hasn't been going too well. Creates itchy trigger fingers," he explained simply before the jeep bounced beneath them and they roared into the compound.

They stopped in front of a forest green canvas tent. Maddie extracted herself from Jack's lap and everyone piled out.

Jack faced his three soldiers. "You guys go have a shower and get some hot chow. Meet me back here at 1900 hours."

"Will do, Sarge," said the driver. The other two men merely nodded their expression unreadable.

Jack turned toward Maddie and Dr. Oz. "I'll take you to see my grandmother."

Maddie nodded and attempted to smooth her rumpled suit with her hands. A few stray hairs fell across her eyes. She blew them away only to see them fall back. She stole a glance at Oz and saw he was trembling, badly shaken by the wild ride.

She patted his shoulder. He looked at her and she smiled at him. "That's what field work is like pretty much all the time. Fun, huh?"

Oz cleared his throat. "Yeah. Fun."

Jack snorted obviously amused by Dr. Oz's reaction. "The general is in this tent," he said, nodding toward the tent the jeep was parked in front of.

They followed Jack inside the tent to find a gray haired woman with the weathered features of someone who'd spent too much time in the sun. The lines on her face reminded Maddie of aged leather. The old woman was seated behind a large ornate oak desk. Her brown eyes looked up from the paper she'd been reading when they entered. When her eyes settled on Jack her weathered features broke into a wide smile. She got up and moved quickly around the desk. She wrapped her arms around Jack and hugged him to her.

After several seconds they broke their hug and she took a step back and gripped his arms with gnarled hands. She gazed into his eyes.

"I heard there was an attack?"

Jack grinned. "No, worries, Gran. Pete got us outta there okay. He's one heck of a driver."

She released Jack from her grip and dropped her arms to her sides. The smile on her face disappeared, only to be replaced by a deep frown.

"Yes, but it means they're close. Too close." She walked around her desk and sat down. "Who are they?"

Jack chuckled. "Sorry. This is ISB Operative Surefoot and Dr. Oz. We found them at Rednose's castle and decided not to leave them to the hostiles."

"For which I and Dr. Oz are very grateful," said Maddie. "General, I must know, what is going on?"

The general gazed at Maddie with dead eyes and her features darkened. "Why were you sent to unreality?"

"With respect, General, I believe I asked a question."

The general leaned forward in her chair and laid her arms flat on the desk. "We are at war with the giants and others, and we don't have a lot of time. Now tell me, why are you here?"

Giants? Plural. There were more than one of them? Oh well, in for a buck in for twenty. "Because of a red shoe that landed in reality."

Maddie frowned. "But what about Rednose? He's a giant."

The general's features softened and her eyes became bright with tears. "He died. When my husband refused to join in with their war they killed him…" Her voice trailed off and she wiped at her eyes with the sleeve of her uniform shirt. Maddie had seen such pain before and decided she'd drop the obviously painful subject.

She cleared her throat and shifted her gaze to Jack. "Is the shoe drop your doing, Sergeant?"

He nodded his mouth a grim line.

The general sighed and eased back in her chair. "We're losing the war, and Jack thought your world might be willing to help."

"What makes you think that?" Maddie frowned at Jack. He grinned sheepishly and her heart fluttered. He was way too handsome for his own good.

"Because, Operative Surefoot, if we lose, your world will be next."

***

Maddie was excited when the general asked Maddie to work with Jack on strategies and plans for counter attack. It would give her chance to know him better.

They stood side by side looking over a waist high table made form sawhorses and plywood. A large map of the battlefields had been spread out on the table and blue and red pins had been used to indicate the coordinates of both sides. Maddie's frown grew deeper the longer she stared at it and realized what it was telling her.

The enemy had broken through their defensive lines in several places. This had resulted in retreating battles between the army of the shoe and the giants and their allies the dwarfs (yes, the irony is not lost on me) and the ogres. Most of the fairytale creatures were with them. An entire village of cookie people and pie makers had declared themselves neutral. So far the enemy had honored their neutrality, but Maddie knew it was only a matter of time before they too were drawn into the war.

Jack stood beside her smelling of soap and cigar smoke. Right now an unlit cigar stuck out from between his gritted teeth. At least he washed. "So what do ya think?" he said.

"You guys are pretty much screwed."

Jack grunted. "Yeah. I know. Any ideas?"

"You mean other than heading for the hills?" She shook her head and emitted a sharp laugh. "But since your pretty much surrounded and the enemy is closing in that ship has sailed."

"So we surrender and hope they don't execute us?"

"Nope. We ask Dr. Oz to build us some weapons. Non-lethal weapons."

She glanced at Jack and saw the arrogant smile had faded and his features had paled. Good, she thought, I threw him a curve ball.

She turned to face him. "Non-lethal weapons will preserve the balance in unreality. If the giants and ogres are all gone then who will rise up and take over?" She arched an eyebrow. "You? The general? The wild unicorns?" Her eyes narrowed. "Or maybe the wizards? We certainly don't want the wizards to take control. That would be very bad and for your world and mine."

Jack's eyes narrowed and he stroked his stubble covered chin with strong fingers. He looked so handsome she had to stop herself from shivering. "I see what you mean." He dropped his hand to his side, his palm now resting off the butt of his pistol in the holster around his narrow waist. "But can Dr. Oz build enough weapons, fast enough to turn the tide of, " with his left hand he swept an arc over the map, "this."

Maddie nodded grimly. "I think we have a month. Dr. Oz can and will do it." Her voice lowered to a whisper. "Or we all die."

***

Maddie rubbed the eyepieces of her gas mask before she stole a look over the wall of sandbags. There they were. The giants were moving across the open field toward their position. The looked warily and slapped their hairy palms with their tree sized wooden clubs.

94

In the last month Dr. Oz had constructed several new classes of weapons for the locals that had taken out several hundred giants and ogres. The fairies and shoe elves had worked night and day to turn out non-lethal bubble guns, and shock cannons, and giggle grenades. These weapons had turned the tide of war in their favor. Maddie was relieved the enemy hadn't changed tactics when the new weapons were deployed and continued to be dependant on their brute force alone.

All that remained of the giants, dwarfs, and ogres army were five giants. The rest of their army had been incapacitated and captured. It was up to her and Jack to take out these last few.

Maddie slipped down once again behind the wall and reached for the box of giggle grenades. She glanced at Jack in his gas mask and they shared an awkward smile.

These giants were going to get a big surprise when they got within range. The incoming giants were causing the ground to tremble beneath the defenders. The earth shook more violently with each deep thud of their massive boot steps as they drew ever closer.

Finally, when Maddie thought they were close enough, she issued the order her troops had been waiting for with a loud yell. "Now!"

She stood up with a grenade in her right hand, Jack did the same. They each pulled the pin, counted to three, and then threw the grenades into the path of the oncoming giants. They dropped down once again behind the sandbags and covered their heads with their arms.

There was a loud bang and the invisible gas dispersed. Maddie heard the giants coughing and the first giggles started. Soon they were laughing uncontrollably. After ten minutes elapsed she heard the five giants fall with thuds so loud she had to cover her ears, her teeth chattered, and the impact made her heart skip a beat.

Maddie began to laugh herself as did Jack. She and Jack had become close and for the first time in along time it seemed she could trust a man again.

Jack turned out to be a kind and gentle man with great passion, and he was a good kisser. But if he was going to win her heart he would have to give up the cigars and shave once in awhile. The latter not too often, of course, she kind of enjoyed the feeling of his stubble on her skin.

After the mop up crews had these remaining giant's secured, and locked in the holding pen to await trial for crimes against unreality, Maddie met with General She-Had-So-Many-Children-She-Didn't-Know-What-To-Do.

They each had a cup of warm mint tea in front of them. "So, my dear, when are you going back?"

"Back?" Maddie sipped her tea.

The general shrugged. "To reality. To your job. Your old life."

Maddie shook her head. "I think I'll stick around for a while."

The general arched one eyebrow. "Oh? Is it my grandson?"

Maddie chuckled. "Yes, partially. But I don't think these giants were alone. I think someone helped them, or incited them. They seem to be puppets of a greater power."

"You may be right." The general's tired eyes dropped to peer at her teacup. A small smile drifted across her pale lips. "I was hoping you'd make an honest man of my grandson."

Maddie lifted her cup to her lips and peered at the old woman over the rim. Before she took another sip she said, "That could be a distinct possibility.

Hard to believe this had all started with one red shoe. Maddie was certain Barb would understand her reasons for staying. She only hoped her mother would.

Five Minutes

BUMP LOOKED UP FROM THE NEWSPAPER he'd been studying into the green-gray eyes of the red haired waitress standing staring expectantly at perfectly cut auburn hair did nothing to disguise she was older than she wanted to be. The oval patch over the sagging left breast of her white uniform blouse read Thelma. He assumed this was her designation.

Bump considered it sad that in his line of work the only women he met had to work past their expiry date and were usually damaged goods. His was a rotten business and sometimes he really hated it. But this particular job meant he had to locate another type of woman. A woman with a deadly agenda.

Only he hoped the woman he'd been paid to find wasn't as world weary as this one. If she was then she wouldn't care about her life or anyone else's. These type of targets were the scariest kind. He really hated those jobs, but a guy had to make a living didn't he?

"What'll it be?" she said her voice rough from too many smoke breaks.

Sometimes he'd forget how many people smoked in the twentieth century. In his day no one smoked. Smoking had been banned long ago.

Too bad he hadn't time before he left to have dummy tobacco sticks made up. He'd have to say he didn't smoke which would put his cover in jeopardy each time he said it. His recollection from his college history class about the middle of the twentieth was everyone smoked. Children as young as five or six started smoking, then they were hooked until they died of smokers cough. At least that was how he remembered it. But he could be mistaken; he wasn't much of a student

Regardless, his plan was he'd be out of here before he had to tell anyone he didn't smoke.

"How 'bout your phone number?" He hoped she didn't say yes because he'd never used a telephone and he had no idea right now how long he'd be in this time.

Her gray eyes narrowed and her mouth formed a sneer. "'Aint on the menu, buster." She stuffed her pad and pencil into the pocket in the front of her apron tied around her waist. She turned around and retrieved a white coffee cup from a stack on a counter under the stainless steel pass bar that separated the cook from the waitress.

On the other side of the open pass bar was the white haired cook in a white cotton undershirt. He sported two missing teeth and hadn't shaved in a couple of days evidenced by the uneven gray stubble on his street weary face. An angry scar ran across his chin and up the left side of his face.

Thelma cocked an eyebrow at him. "Coffee?"

Bump smiled. "Yeah. Sure. Thanks."

She snorted as she turned her back to him. "Don't be thanking me until you've tasted this mud."

"You watch yor mouth, T," said the cook gruffly from the kitchen.

The coffee shop was empty at this time of day. Evidently no one fancied greasy spoon food at three in the morning.

Thelma smirked and selected a white porcelain cup from a stack next to the large steel coffee percolator on the counter then held the cup under a spigot and filled the cup with black coffee. She set the full cup in front of him. His nose wrinkled at the smell of over cooked beans cut with too much chicory.

He recognized the smell from his days in the marines when he was stationed in the outer worlds. They used to cheap out the military in those days. The days before the second great war. A buddy who'd stayed in sent him an e-note once telling him how jarheads ate steak every night and drank gourmet coffee.

Bump never heard from the guy again so he assumed he'd become fodder in the seemingly endless war to end all wars. At least he left on a full stomach topped off with some decent coffee. Not like this foul swill was sure to taste.

He folded the newspaper in half and laid it on the coffee counter and searched the counter for the sugar and salt and peppershakers. There were none in evidence. "Sugar?"

"You're kiddin' right?"

He remembered now. Milk, sugar, flour and salt were rationed but he didn't remember why. And he couldn't recall at the moment who the enemy in this war had been. He glanced at the headline on the folded newspaper. Duhhh. Nazi's. Of course.

"Do you have any milk?" he said politely as possible

A sardonic smile played across her lips and she went to a large refrigerator standing at the end of the counter shoved against a wall next to the swinging door to the back. She came back with a glass bottle half filled with milk.

She tipped it and whitened his coffee. He smiled at her. "Thanks."

'Where you from, mister?" Thelma said when she came back from putting the milk bottle away.

Oh, oh. Now what? "Why would you think I'm not from around here?" he said keeping his voice as even as possible.

She eyed him suspiciously. "You talk funny and your clothes are wrong."

Bump sat back against the back of the chair and chuckled. "Well, well how 'bout that. Nothing gets past you does it, Thelma?"

She scowled at him and looked about to leap across the counter at him. He'd insulted her. He'd never been skilled at sarcasm. Not good. She'd soon begin to think he was a Nazi too.

"Sorry. What I meant was you're right. I'm visiting. I'm from Chicago." It was a lie but certainly preferable to the truth.

Thelma's features softened. "American, eh? What ya doin' here?"

"I'm a private investigator. I'm trying to locate someone. Name's Bump McShott."

Thelma turned her head toward the kitchen and yelled, "Hey, Archie, Sam Spade is in the shop."

"Tell him he's gotta order sumthin' like everybody else," called Archie from the kitchen.

Thelma offered him a thin smile. "Archie don't go to the movies much."

Bump wondered what a movie was and who how he'd been mistaken for a guy named Sam Spade. He thought about correcting her but her eyes had the spark that meant he'd found his way in to her camp. Problem was he had no idea what a movie was.

He made a mental note in future he should do better research before coming this far back. Unfortunately, this job's timeline didn't allow sufficient time to do the necessary research.

All he'd been able to do was find a vessel to inhabit for the twenty-four hours he needed to track Pinky Ames and to stop her.

The time table said he'd only have five minutes after he found ted her but his one strong asset was over confidence born of success. It was why he accepted the hefty payday, if he achieved the objective. His business was result based so it was feast or famine. And famine usually meant paradoxes for someone. So far he hadn't created any personal paradoxes, at least none he was aware of.

He smiled at Thelma and took a sip from the warm coffee mug. He winced when the acidic brew burned his tongue. He was thankful when his taste buds were burned because it meant he couldn't taste the stuff. He'd drunk coffee during other assignments and the stuff was an acquired taste he'd never acquired.

Thelma leaned her elbows on the counter and stared at him with a thin smile on her lips. "You're not from Chicago are you, Bump?"

He believed the popular jargon of the period in this circumstances' went; 'The jig is up.' He had no idea what a jig was but somehow it fit this situation. "No. Not Chicago," he said slowly, keeping his eyes fixed on hers.

Thelma straightened up after removing her elbows from the counter then crossed her arms over her bosom. "I know who you are because I'm also not from Chicago." She nodded toward Archie who was visible over the stainless steel pass bar in the kitchen. "And neither is Archie."

"What year?" Bump asked. It was along shot but something about the way they talked told him they were out of period too.

A shadow of a smile played across her lips and her eyes narrowed. "2434. You?"

"2418," Bump replied. "Kinda crowded in the past these days don't ya think?"

101

Thelma smirked. "Yeah. Sure is." Her brow wrinkled. "Corporate, government, or private?"

Bump set the mug on the counter then reached over ad pulled a paper napkin from the dispenser. He wiped his mouth with the napkin then crumpled it in his fist. "Private. Like I said I'm a private investigator."

Thelma's thick, dark eyebrows formed twin arches on her forehead. "Really? You really a PI?" He nodded. She chuckled and shook her head. "Me and Miles are on holiday. You sure look the part in that rain coat and the fedora."

Bump grinned. These two were rich morons on a lark.

Somewhere in their program was an automatic retrieval worm if they tried to change history. Any attempt to assassinate Hitler, or provide future technology to someone in the past resulted in automatic retrieval, a hefty fine and prosecution. There had been a few cases where the death penalty had been handed out, but most often the offender was subjected to a memory wipe.

Since the entire purpose of vacation time travel was to see and interact with the past, and share the experiences at parties, a memory wipe was considered a sufficient deterrent.

The idle rich were the customers of the time travel corporations so they stayed in line with the rules.

Bump had lost count of the number of times he wished for a memory wipe, but while his trips were privately funded they were hardly vacations so he was allowed some leniency in the application of the rules. And the Time Enforcement Agency had thus far been unable to tie him into any disruption to the timeline. The corporations who hired him had friends in high places to take care of his missteps.

Bump reached into the pocket inside his suit jacket and pulled out a black and white photograph.

He showed the smiling woman depicted in the photograph to Thelma.

"You seen her in here? Or has anyone mentioned an Arlene Bennett to either of you."

This diner was near the debarkation wharf where the troop and cargo vessels docked to refuel and load with men and material for war. Just about every sailor that had ever come through the port had come into this diner. Bump assumed this was why Thelma (obviously not her real name) and Miles (disguised as Archie) wanted to be here. They'd get a wealth of experiences from the sailors who came through to brag about at parties.

Surprisingly Thelma scoffed. "Archie, get out here."

She must have become accustomed to using her companions cover name because she sneered it in the sincere way people who believed what they were saying. These two had clearly done their research before coming back.

Bump stuffed the picture of Arlene Bennett back inside his suit jacket just as Archie came through the swinging door. A grease stained white apron covered his clothes and trails of dirty sweat streaked his puffy freckled cheeks. Sitting atop a nest of tight oil-black curls he wore a round white hat. His jaw was tight with undisguised anger.

Bump swallowed hard. This man was a tough customer.

Thelma looked at him with a sneer ion her face. "Throw this guy out, Arch."

"What? Why?" said Bump. He remained seated as Archie rounded the end of the counter and came at him. He realized he wasn't getting an explanation when Archie spun the stool around and grabbed by him shirt collar and his belt and yanked him to his feet. Spots danced before his eyes due to the sudden application of force to his windpipe.

Bump estimated Archie had a good fifteen kilos on him so he knew struggling would be pointless, and would likely result in a black eye or a broken bone or two. Any serious injuries would delay his mission and he'd miss his window of opportunity. Missing an assignment was unacceptable to his employer and would result in disciplinary action.

He smiled to himself. Too bad discipline meant a single shot to the head. Not that he was worried; his success rate of one hundred percent and holding was in the corporations and his best interest to maintain. The corporations didn't wish to attract unwanted attention from the certain government agencies if his assignments went awry. Of course he'd be the one to suffer the most but any corporation with a prohibition to mine the past would soon enter bankruptcy. The arrangement was symbiotic but deadly in its implications.

Archie raised so his feet no longer touched the floor and carried him toward the front door of the diner.

Bump gagged and sputtered waving his arms as the heavily muscled time traveler-slash-cook carried him to the door. Once at the door he was dangled in mid air for what seemed to be an eternity. His vision blurred as a lack of oxygen starved his brain. He heard Thelma heels click on the dirty tile floor until she came into view and swung the door open. She offered a tight lipped smile and waved her fingers at him just before Archie tossed him out the door where he landed hard on his butt on the rain soaked sidewalk.

He gasped for air and spots danced in front of his eyes as he managed to drag the first few breathes into his tortured lungs. Slowly his breathing normalized. His butt was wet and it hurt like hell.

His day wasn't going as he'd planned that much was clear. But unanticipated violence was in the job description.

After managing to stand on shaky legs he stumbled into the alley across the street from the diner.

Daybreak was still several hours away so he had little concern he'd run into trouble in the alley.

With his mind now clear, Bump decided to stay where he was to observe who arrived in the diner after his abrupt departure. The alley was shrouded in shadow so he wouldn't be seen by anyone walking by.

In contrast the diner was well lit from inside. He would have a perfect view of anyone coming and going in the diner. Her saw Thelma and Archie moving about their movements frantic and nervous. They reminded him of birds in a cage. It seemed they had lost their courage after their rough treatment of him.

Right now they were looking mostly to the west toward a row of three story brick apartments farther down the street. Evidently, something about Arlene Bennett had unnerved them.

He didn't have to wait long because a woman wearing a scarf over her dirty blonde hair appeared huddled in a long wool overcoat rushing toward the diner. She entered through the diner's door. The echo of tinny bell over the door drifted on the cold winter air to him standing in the alley. He shivered.

The woman was immediately met by Thelma and Archie who appeared highly agitated given how they spoke rapidly and waved their hands about to as if to emphasize what they were saying. Now he understood his treatment. These two were conspirators with Arlene Bennett and this woman had to be Arlene, the subject of his investigation.

Bump considered bursting into the diner and apprehending her but this would not stop whatever plans her employer had in mind, he or she would just send someone else. And he'd not discover the identity of the person who hired her. His information was a corporation had hired her, she wasn't an agent of an official body.

Now raised, angry voices drifted through the windows of the diner. Bump smiled to himself. His appearance had upset their plans. "Good," he mused under his breath.

Finally Arlene left the diner, after slamming the door hard behind she walked briskly headed toward the row brick apartment buildings that abutted the dock area.

Bump stepped out of the alley and began to follow her keeping a discrete distance between them. He ducked into another alley when Arlene stopped to look for anyone following her. He held his breath and stole a quick look around the wall and to see she once again had started walking. He started after her keeping his distance and using any shadows he encountered to cover his tailing her.

They had walked nearly an hour and were in an area of the city unfamiliar to him. The buildings were still made of brick, mortar and stone but they were higher and more ornately decorated along the roofline with scrolls and carved stone statues of gargoyles and other mythic creatures.

Finally they arrived at the apparent destination because Arlene entered one of the buildings using a key she pulled from her coat pocket.

She closed the door behind her and he heard the echo of the lock being turned.

Bump waited several seconds then rushed to the door. As he suspected it was locked.

He grunted softly in frustration then scanned the street to see if anyone was watching him. Delivery trucks had started moving on the streets but there were no pedestrians on the sidewalks at this still early hour.

Looking back to peer at the lock in the door handle, Bump reached into the pocket of his overcoat and pulled out a small red disc-shaped object. He placed the disc over the keyhole in the door and there was a soft click. Taking one last look both right and left at the street and seeing no one he swung the door inward and, after pocketing the disc, slipped inside closing and locking the door behind him. He had to be careful not to let anyone of this period see the lock pick.

Since he had no idea where in the twenty story building Arlene would be he decided to check the directory to see if he recognized any names from the thin briefing file he'd been provided. Naturally he'd used his usual back door sources to augment what he was provided, and to determine exactly whom he was working for. He needed to know of the true objective of his mission.

Bump hadn't survived fifteen years in this business without discovering the hidden agenda of his employer. He was fairly sure every corporation that hired him knew he did this but they never said anything since he got results.

In the low light coming form the beginnings of dawn coming through the lobby windows he Bump scanned the names listed alphabetically on a brass plate set in the wall between the two elevators.

His heart froze and he took in a breath when he came to a name he recognized. Robert Shaw, MD, Room 1012.

Dr. Shaw was the ancestor of his employer, Hart Shaw CEO of Light Drive Technologies. Arlene was here to kill Dr. Shaw. But why?

***

When he arrived at the office door of Dr. Shaw, Bump saw there was light coming from under the door. The rest of the building was deserted so this had to be where Arlene had come.

Resting his ear against the door he managed to make out muffled voices. Good. Arlene hadn't left so Dr. Shaw must still be alive.

Bump slowly tried turning the doorknob, but like the lobby door it too was locked. He cursed under his breath. The elevator motors broke the silence startling him. His heart beat rapidly and his mouth dried.

He was running out of time the early starters had begun to arrive. Bump ran his tongue across his lower lips then took out the lock disc and placed it on the Dr. Shaw's door lock.

It was risky to burst into the room. If Arlene had a weapon trained on Dr. Shaw she'd kill him before he could stop her. And then his employer would be gone and then a paradox for him and death for a whole line of Shaw's and who knew how many others. He would need toy proceed with caution, even if it meant his own death.

Bump heard the lock disengage then he slowly swung to door in. The light inside went out.

"Hello?" he said as the door opened. "Dr. Shaw?"

"Come in and close the door behind you," said a husky woman's voice. It must be Arlene.

As Bump's eyesight adjusted to the low light coming through drawn shades over the windows the shrouded image of a someone standing next to a chair with another person seated became distinguishable.

"Dr. Shaw?" he said again.

"Dr. Shaw is tied up at the moment. What do you want?"

"Uhhh, I need some medical advice."

Arlene chuckled mockingly. "Yeah. Nice try. Dr. Shaw isn't a medical doctor so you may as well leave."

Bump smiled to himself. "Sorry, you and I both know I can't do that." Bump moved to the right side of the door and found a light switch on the wall.

He flicked the switch and the overhead light in the middle of the ceiling. He blinked and recognized Dr. Shaw seated on a wooden chair. His arms were tied to the chair with black electrical cord and a cloth had been stuffed in his mouth. Bump recognized him because his future great, great, great grandson looked exactly like him.

He hadn't been harmed but that was about to change. On the floor underneath the chair was a bomb, a bomb he recognized. When it went off it would implode everything within five feet. Since it was designed to implode upward Dr. Shaw so he would disappear forever. It would be like he never existed which seemed poetic.

"How long?" he said simply gazing into Arlene's eyes.

Her eyes were dark as a pool of water at night and her expression was placid, unconcerned. Her attitude unnerved him. But he was determined not to show she'd gotten to him.

"It has a five minute timer. We have four minutes and thirty eight seconds to get out."

He knew exactly what she meant. They'd leave these bodies that would be consumed by the blast and their own consciousness would return to their own time. It concerned him that he and Arlene might not exist in the future since the timeline would have been altered, but that was the risk of corporate espionage in the past.

Sometimes he wondered what reality was anymore. With all the time travel going on reality had probably changed so many times that truth had little meaning.

He and Arlene could have played out this cat and mouse game many times, and every time the result would have been different.

"What corporation you working for?" he asked to keep the conversation going. By his mental calculation they had four minutes and thirteen seconds.

Her mouth formed a half smile. "Not working for them."

He nodded at the terrified Shaw who struggled to free his arms. The chair rocked side to side. With sufficient time he'd probably have gotten free but there wasn't time. "Then why?"

Her eyes became hard and her mouth became a grim line. "Personal reasons."

Bump arched an eyebrow. "Really? Tell me."

"Why should I?"

"Well, for one reason in three minutes and forty one seconds we're all going to die or you and I will disappear in a paradox. So I say why not?"

Surprisingly, she smiled. "Sure. Why not?"

A bead of sweat trickled down Bumps shirt collar.

Three minutes and fifteen seconds.

"Dr. Shaw will have three sons. Two become doctors, psychiatrists like himself, while the third becomes a train engineer. These three men marry and each have two children. Of these the records are somewhat murky due to a paradox but our record does show one boy grows up to found a black market munitions company."

"So his ancestor killed your family, right?" interrupted Bump.

She scowled at him. "Don't be ridiculous. Do you want to hear the story or not?"

Two minutes and thirty-one seconds.

"Yeah, sure. Sorry."

"So, as I was saying my father —"

"Your father?" He couldn't help himself.

"Yes," she crossed her arms over her chest. "My father's company was founded as a munitions company selling arms to the highest bidder. The money made is tainted with innocent blood."

"So you want to clear your conscience is that it?"

"No, it's too late for that."

"But your father's company now manufacturers faster than light drives and has helped humanity to travel the stars and open up trade with countless worlds across the galaxy. That's not so bad is it?"

One minute and twenty-five seconds.

"Unless you've seen the future then I would say you're correct."

Bumps heart froze. Travel to the future was illegal and highly dangerous. Tampering with future events could have disastrous consequences for the past.

She smiled.

One minute and one second.

"What has Dr. Shaw got to do with this?"

"As I said he will have three sons."

So that was it. Wipe Dr. Shaw from existence, no children, and no Shaw's, including Arlene, or whatever her name was.

Forty-one seconds.

"You know you'll be gone too, right?" She nodded. Then he realized she wasn't leaving before the implosion.

Thirty-eight seconds.

He fought the urge to ask her what she'd seen in the future but he knew in his gut he didn't want to know. No one should know. What he did know was Arlene was willing to sacrifice herself to save the future.

Twenty-nine seconds.

He paced the room. "I have to know, Arlene."

"My name's Ariel Shaw actually," she said.

Twenty-five seconds.

"Well then, Ariel I have to be sure I'm doing the right thing."

"I know I'm right. I saw it with my own eyes," she said.

Bump gazed into her eyes. Does he trust her? He had to do what was right.

Eighteen seconds.

Bump looked at Dr. Shaw and saw the raw fear in his eyes. He blinked away the sweat trickling into his eyes. Did he deserve to die to save the future? Did anyone?

Eleven seconds.

"How about I take Dr. Shaw back with me?" Bump suggested.

"Is that even possible?"

He shook his head. "No."

Eight seconds.

"Are you going to stop me?" Ariel asked.

"No." In truth he hadn't fully decided.

Three seconds.

With one second to go Bump decided. He triggered the return worm in the program and woke up in the travel chamber.

He breathed a sigh of relief. He was still here. No paradox. As he stepped out of the chamber and headed for the showers since he'd been in the chamber for the past twenty-four hours.

The memory of the last twenty-four hours began to fade as he stood under the spray of the hot shower. By the time he finished it was gone.

All it took was five minutes and the past was gone forever.

Bump looked forward to his next assignment and wondered where and when it would take him.

Children of the Monster

I STOOD SHIVERING IN FRONT OF THE MASSIVE OAK DOOR staring with fascination at the devils head doorknocker the size of a small terrier. The ornate iron ornament was at eye level in the center of the scarred wood. My mentor, friend and, like I, professional Pinkerton's agent, Noel Stoker stood next to me on the stone stoop.

I must have been out of my mind when I agreed to accompany Noel to a cold, dank and smelly village named Limberburger. The Baron Frankenstein sent us a letter requesting we come to his castle?

Noel must have thought I'm a fool to believe such nonsense.

I'd rather hoped Limberburger was a pub in Soho. I buried my ice-cold hands in the pockets of my coat.

Jokes on me. Ha, ha...

Noel must have known of the cold mists that swirl through this valley in early winter. He was wearing his father's thick wool topcoat and heavy gloves. His balding head was covered with his favorite grey felt fedora. I on the other hand wore my thinner fall trench coat. I was dressed for London drizzle not Limberburger winter.

Noel glanced at me his hazel eyes impatient then grasped the heavy knocker and pounded it against the door once, then twice more in rapid succession. Thunderous thumps greeted our ears as the sound of metal on wood echoed from the other side of the massive door. Then a voice thick and gruff and edged with sleep called out from behind the door.

"I'm coming for goodness sake! What's your hurry! How'm I supposed to get my beauty sleep?"

The mist swirled about my ankles like spider webs as we waited.

After several seconds I heard the sounds of numerous locks being sprung and latches being let loose. I took one step back as the door finally swung inward. Its steel hinges squealed due to centuries of rust.

The man — well not a man exactly, for his face, was misshapen as if it were made of clay had one eye socket set lower than the other. The nose, which was as crooked as a mountain trail, was narrow with a bump in the middle. His skin was pale almost translucent and his eyes were of two different colors, one brown and one green — greeted us with a grunt and a look of distain.

In a right hand larger than is normal for a man of his diminutive stature he held a silver candleholder with three receptacles. The three candles in the receptacles were lit and the golden flames cast long shadows across the darkened entrance. I could feel the heat that emanated from the candles from where I stood on the stone stoop. He smells of cheese. And he's a hunchback.

"Yes! What do you want?"

Noel, ever the gentleman of regal propriety, bowed slightly at the waist and tipped his hat. "We are seeking an audience with the Baron Frankenstein. We have come some distance at his request."

Noel reached into the inside pocket of his suit jacket within the folds of the great coat and withdrew the letter we received a fortnight ago at our offices in London.

The Baron had written us seeking our assistance in locating a valuable object'd art. At least that's what Noel told our boss, Mr. Thomas. I didn't believe him but Mr. Thomas seemed pleased to get rid of us. At least that's what his grunt seemed to convey.

With a twist of the tip of his waxed moustache Noel handed the letter to the gnarled dwarf.

"My name is Noel Stoker, and this is my colleague Denis Doyle. We represent the Pinkerton Detective Agency."

The hunchback eyed the letter skeptically then sighed heavily and stepped back. "Come in."

Noel shot me a wink then stepped through the doorway. Once inside the hunchback closed the heavy door and I watched enthralled as he re-engaged all of the numerous locks.

They're certainly security conscious around here.

He must have seen my interest in this activity. "You can never be too careful. There are children of the night who would roam this valley. Sometimes they come home very late."

The interior was cloaked in inky darkness but in the dim light I could make out the wide spiral staircase made of mahogany that disappeared upward into the gloom.

I shivered again. Not from fear but due to the draft of cold air that washed over us. The evil looking dwarf didn't seem to notice the cold though he was dressed in only a nightshirt, and sleeping cap. I looked at his feet and was surprised to see he was wearing large fuzzy bunny slippers.

How odd.

"My master will be down shortly."

"How does he know we're here?" I blurted.

The hunchback's twisted features became a smile I would not want to see twice in my lifetime. The creature's yellow crooked teeth and grotesque mouth would have repulsed even father's famed fictional detective.

Noel nodded. "Thank you, Igor."

The dwarf frowned. "Name's Herman. Igor was my father."

Noel grinned and twisted his moustache as his dark eyes scanned the dimly lit surroundings. "Yes, of course."

Herman the hunchback grunted and walked to a side table where there was another of the three candle stick holders and used the one he carried to light the candles. He then turned and shuffled to the spiral staircase. It was then I noticed his left leg was withered and he had to drag it behind him.

No wonder it took him so long to come to the door. Noel must have had the same thought because he eyed me knowingly and nodded toward Herman who had started to climb the stairs. "Good night... Ig...I mean, Herman."

Herman stopped and looked back over his shoulder at a grinning Noel. "The master will be down shortly." He soon disappeared into a door at the top of the stairs.

I fidgeted as the sound of a wolf howl was carried with the cold draft. "Spooky place uh, Noel?"

Noel smiled. "Yes. Quite."

"Do you think the Baron Frankenstein is —"

"— The model for Mary Shelly's monster?" One eyebrow arched up Noel's forehead and there was a twinkle in his eye. I nodded as I pulled the flaps around the collar of my trench coat tighter around my neck.

Noel shrugged. "Probably. I know my father seemed to think so." His eyes narrowed. "Of course my father used a fifteenth century Transylvanian Prince as his model for his book, so I'm not surprised that Shelly would use a Limberburger Baron. There are numerous legends surrounding this castle."

"Yes there are, Mr. Stoker."

I looked around for the source of the voice and realized it came from the top of the staircase. In the darkness I could make out a human figure.

"Baron Frankenstein, I presume?" Noel moved to the half moon shaped side table and picked up the candleholder. He carried it the bottom of the stairs and squinted into the darkness as the meager light from the candles made the shadows retreat so that the Baron's features were somewhat invisible.

Now I know, dear reader you are expecting a description of pure horror. An apparition of a ghoul harvested from dead flesh. But what met my eyes was a man of medium height, with thinning brown hair receded on a pale forehead dressed in a tattered forest green bathrobe, while scuffed black leather slippers adorned his feet. His eyes were beady and his legs bandy.

He reminded me more of a factory worker from the midlands than creature nightmares are made of. If this was indeed Dr. Frankenstein's creation then Mary Shelly was far from accurate in her depiction of him.

The Baron buried his hands in the pockets of his bathrobe then started down the stairs. "I'm glad you made it. I didn't expect you so soon, or so late."

He stopped at the bottom of the staircase a half smile on his lips. His black eyes were watchful. "You should have waited until morning to come out to the castle.

Herman is quite right about things that go bump in the night you know."

I looked to Noel to take the lead. He cleared his throat. "Of course, Baron, but we are here and are ready and able to start our investigation immediately."

The Baron smirked. "I suppose you're wondering about the object I spoke of in my letter."

"Yes, sir we are curious." I chimed in.

Noel glared at me then his features relaxed. "Yes, Baron. That as well with your knowledge of the region who the potential suspects might be," Noel said.

The Baron smiled. "If I had told you in the letter what to expect you would never have accepted the case." He paused his eyes thoughtful. "Why don't we go into the library? We'll be more comfortable in there. I believe there have been provisions made for our comfort."

I glanced toward the top of the stairs where Herman had disappeared through the door. How had our host made provisions when his manservant had obviously returned to bed?

The Baron turned on his heel and walked toward a door off the foyer. It was closed but as we approached I could make out a polished brass plaque affixed to the door with the words Dr. Frankenstein's library in raised black letters.

The Baron tapped the plaque with his index finger. "For the tourists. Herman conducts tours of the castle in the summer." The Baron opened the door and held it for Noel and I as we entered. He closed the behind him once we were all inside.

"Since that God awful film last year we have seen a steady growth in the curious and the zealots." He rolled his eyes.

The library was a magnificent homage to the written word for a bibliophile like me.

The built in bookcases rose from floor level to the ceiling some twenty feet over our heads.

Noel snuffed out the candles because at the far end of the room interrupting the shelf of books was a floor-to-ceiling stone fireplace complete with a roaring fire. I gazed at the cracking blue, yellow and red flames and felt the chill begin to leave my frigid body.

In front of the fireplace was an antique Chinese silk rug. In the middle of the rug was an octagon-shaped rosewood coffee table surrounded by four leather wing backed chairs.

"What took you so long, darling?" A slender woman wearing a simple navy blue skirt and a white blouse, with dark curls tired in a loose knot that flowed down her left side, rose from one of the wing chairs and smiled warmly. Her pale grey eyes were as warm as the fire.

"I'm sorry, my love." The Baron smiled in kind. "You know me. I had to make my dramatic entrance."

The woman laughed brightly. "I'm sorry, gentleman. My husband can be such a bore."

Noel stepped forward after removing his fedora and took the woman's hand in his then leaned forward and kissed it lightly. "It is an honor, Baroness."

She smiled at him after he let go of her hand and straightened. "I met your father once. It was summer in Geneva..." she paused and looked thoughtful for a second. "Yes. It was the summer of 1894."

1894? She appeared to be no older than thirty. The mystery deepens.

Noel appeared unfazed by this revelation. With a wave of her fine boned hand the Baroness indicated we should sit across from her. The Baron sat in the wing chair next to hers. We took our seats and now faced the Baron and Baroness Frankenstein. Let me tell you, dear reader it was a surreal moment to be sure.

"I'm sorry," Noel, indicated me. "I should introduce Denis Doyle, my fellow agent."

The Baroness looked delighted. "How wonderful! Imagine the son of the author of those mesmerizing tales of Sherlock Holmes in our library." She patted her husband's hand. "Isn't this extraordinary, darling."

"Yes, dear it is indeed. But these gentlemen are here on a mission of grave importance." He paused and his features visibly flushed. "I make it all sound so trivial."

Noel's expression became serious his eyes attentive. "Maybe now's the time to tell us what this is about, Baron."

The Baron sighed and nodded. He sat back heavily in the chair while the Baroness went to a sideboard where a silver tea service sat. She lifted the tray and brought it to the rosewood coffee table where she set it down. Like any good hostess she began to serve tea to each in turn.

The Baron started to tell his tale.

"After the original Baron died he bequeathed this castle, all its possessions, and his title to me, his creation. Since my only name was The Monster I assumed his family name as my own." The Baroness sat down with a cup of tea in her hand just as the Baron gazed at the delicate creature with her high cheekbones, perfect posture and skin the color of alabaster.

"My wife is also the Baron's creation. She is my BFF."

"BFF?" I asked.

A thin smile crossed the Baron's lips. "Bride of Frankenstein Forever." The expression in his eyes turned cold. "And when I say forever I mean it literally. I assure you eternity is a long time." Silence interrupted only by the crackle of the burning wood in the fireplace filled the room.

Noel edged forward on his chair and took a sip of the fragrant tea. "Please continue."

The Baron's eyes shifted to Noel. "Elizabeth and I could not sire a child though we desperately wanted one. We thought if there were others of our kind then our loneliness would be cured."

"You didn't…" I breathed. Noel shot me a scathing look to silence me.

The Baron shook his head. "Not at first. We tried every medical specialist in the known world." She shook his head sadly. "But it was all for naught until…."

"Until?" Noel looked as if he was about to fall off the edge of his chair he had slid so far forward.

"We turned to the source we knew would help us achieve our dream." The Baron stood and walked to a shelf of tall volumes. "There used to be two volumes of his journal, until volume two went missing several months ago."

He plucked a book off the shelf and carried it with both hands, owing to its considerable size and weight, to the coffee table. His wife moved the tray to allow sufficient space for the large, thick book. The Baron placed the book on the table with a soft thump and opened it to the first page.

There in ornate handwriting was the evidence that science had indeed triumphed over death. The Baron's tale was confirmed. This was Victor Frankenstein's record of how he had reanimated dead tissue. And these two beings before me were such creations.

Dizziness came over me as I realized I had been conversing with reanimated bodies. Or rather if the legend were true pieces of bodies sewn together and shot through with electrical energy until they came to life. It was too terrible to imagine.

Upon seeing my distress the Baroness leapt to her feet and rushed to my side. She placed a comforting hand on my shoulder. Her brow was wrinkled with concern.

How sweet she is. If only she weren't an undead ghoul. She cast an annoyed look at the Baron her eyes scolded him.

The Baron sighed stood and rested his hand on the mantel over the fireplace. He stared at the fire.

"Please accept my apology, Mr. Doyle. What you think we are and what we truly are very different things. Yes, we are creations but not in the way that Hollywood debacle portrayed us. We are not comprised of sewn together corpses."

His words did not lessen my revulsion of these creatures.

"We were born like you but we died during a cholera epidemic in…" he paused. "Excuse me, the year is unimportant. The important thing is Baron Frankenstein revived us and gave us new life. Eternal life."

"But what about the child?" Noel spoke with fervor in his voice.

"Yes, we did revive a child using the Baron's notes in this journal." He paused and the edges of his eyes sagged. "Then we did it again."

I looked wide-eyed at my colleague. "There are two of them?"

"Boy and girl?" asked Noel. The Baron nodded.

Noel leaned toward me and whispered "Salt and pepper."

I looked at him quizzically. "What?"

"Boy and girl. Salt and pepper. Get it?"

I did but I shrugged my shoulders as if I didn't. Noel frowned at me. He turned to face the Baron once again. "So what seems to be at the heart of the problem?"

The Baron rolled his eyes. "We're married with monsters."

I looked around nervously. "Where are they now?"

The Baroness Elizabeth Frankenstein patted my shoulder then walked to her chair and sat again. "Bolt and Stitch are missing. We need your help to find them. That's why we decided to hire you."

***

Children of the vat. At least that's what the Baron called them. They were out somewhere in the world, and the only lead we had was a picture of Bolt and Stitch's high school graduating class. The names of the smiling teenagers in the photo were written on the back.

If the teenage son and daughter of the monster were in the picture I was curious what they'd look like. I looked at the smiling youthful faces and did not see any difference between them. They all appeared fully human.

I flipped the picture over the scanned the names. No Frankenstein's, and no one with the colorful names of Bolt or Stitch.

The two devilish children had been missing for three months with no word. The local constabulary had refused to look for the monstrous offspring given their origin and that of their parents. The Frankenstein's had written to every detective agency in Europe and America with a please for help. We had been the only ones crazy enough to respond.

Great, Noel, what have you gotten us into?

I gazed at the picture and read the names on the back of the picture in earnest as Noel took notes. I didn't say anything until Noel and I were in the coach headed back into the village.

"I know one of those names."

Noel looked at me in surprise. When I didn't speak his eyes narrowed. "Well, man out with it. Who?"

"Val Koptnik." I looked smug in my conviction.

Noel frowned. "Who is Val Koptnik?"

"Only the richest man in Limberburger. He owns the local cheese fac...tor...y..." My words petered out as I connected the dots in my mind.

Herman smelled of cheese...Koptnik owns the cheese factory.... volume two of the mad doctors journal is missing...

"How do you know any of this, Doyle?"

"I read about it in the Times."

Noel eyes were wide with surprise. "The Times? The Times of London had an article about a Limberburger cheese manufacturer?"

I shook my head. "In the Limberburger Times on the train while you were sleeping."

"Oh. Quite."

I frowned. "What is it?" asked Noel frustrated with my manner.

"We haven't a moment to lose. We must to get to the cheese factory before it's too late."

Noel scoffed. "Cheese factory? Why? Are you hungry?"

I shook my head just as the coach bounced on the pot holed filled country road. My head struck the roof of the carriage with a sharp snap. I winced and rubbed the sore spot on my crown. "No. Owww...I think... I've found the resolution to this case."

I closed my eyes. It was too terrible to contemplate. "And I think what we'll find at that factory is the stuff nightmares are made of."

With one hand still on my wounded head I stood hunched over, so as not to hit the roof of the carriage, and stuck my head out the window. "Driver...take us to the Koptnik Cheese Factory."

***

The carriage driver left us as soon as we arrived at the cheese factory. No doubt the odor was the deciding factor for his hasty departure.

Not that I blame him.

I pulled out my handkerchief and held it over my nose and mouth.

"Cough. I guess you get used to the smell, eh Doyle?" Noel led the way in the darkness toward a door lit by a bare bulb in a steel fixture hung off a metal pole.

Once at the door I tested the knob. It turned easily. I nodded to Noel and opened the door as quietly as possible. The hinges must have been oiled regularly because the door opened without a sound. I felt the tension in my shoulders ease.

Good so far.

I stepped inside first and Noel followed close behind. The door was on a spring because it closed just as softly behind us. The lights inside were of low wattage bathing the interior in a soft glow. Banks of large steel pipes ran side by side the length of the ceiling toward the center of the plant. Ahead of us in the dim light I could see a steel railing and stairs that led to a lower level. I walked toward the railing and waved to Noel to follow.

Once at the railing we were met by a sea of massive vats of bubbling liquids. The color of the liquid was different in each. Several shades of red, blue, and yellow were represented.

Primary colors...interesting.

A sudden movement at the corner of my eye made me flinch. But my reaction was too slow. A sharp blow to the head and darkness engulfed me.

***

My head throbbed as I regained consciousness. My head swam from the pain that shot across my forehead and down my neck. I tried to move my arms but realized was tied to a chair by thick ropes. To my right sat Noel also secured by ropes to a chair. He was still unconscious.

125

"How do you feel?"

I looked around me for the source of the voice and saw a figure in the shadows just outside the cone of light from the bulb that hung over our heads.

"Bolt Frankenstein?"

The figure stepped into the light. My jaw dropped. Bolt had to be at least seventy and was probably much older than that. In accordance with the legends chronological age had little to do with the reality of these manmade creatures.

"Yes. I'm Bolt." He was dressed in ash-grey coveralls and a matching work shirt. His hair was snow white and his face narrow with azure intense eyes. "How do you know me?"

"Your parents engaged me and my partner." With a nod of my head that caused me to wince I indicated Noel. "We're Pinkerton detectives."

A woman dressed identically to Bolt whom I assumed to be Stitch stepped from the shadows. "They don't care about us. They only care about their precious book." She cocked one eyebrow at me. "He wants the journal. Not us."

Bolt who until now had his hands buried in the pockets of his coveralls removed his right hand and with a snub nosed nickel-plated revolver.

Oh, oh…I think we're in real trouble. Boy is Noel going to kill me for getting us killed.

"No, Bolt, put the gun away." Stitch stepped beside her brother and placed her hand on the gun and eased the barrel down. Bolt looked venom at me, but did as she instructed. "We create life we don't take it. We're not like the Baron."

"So it's true?" I was pleased with myself. I had figured it out. If we left here alive, Noel would have to be proud of me.

Stitch nodded. "Yes, we're creating a new race. It was the dream of Victor Frankenstein to create a race of supermen and we're going to make that dream a reality."

"No, daughter you are not." The Baron and Baroness stepped out of the shadows behind us.

Great. I'm surrounded by ageless monsters who are embroiled in a family dispute. This can't be a good thing.

Stitch screamed and Bolt lifted the pistol and a shot rang out. The light over my head went out casting the room into inky darkness.

I heard grunts and yelling then footsteps running. More angry shouts in the distance then silence.

"Hey, Doyle...what's going?" Noel was finally awake.

"I'll fill you in later, Noel. Right now we have to find a way to get untied..."

"I'm not tied."

After Noel managed to find me in the darkness he untied me and after getting lost several times we finally found the room with the massive vats of bubbling liquids and made our way to the staircase.

Once outside and after an hour of walking we were arrived at the Pigs Snout Tavern.

The next day we boarded a train and headed for London and home.

Along the way I explained the events at the cheese factory to Noel and we agreed we would not be getting paid. In fact, Mr. Thomas would very likely fire us both.

Fortunately, Mr. Thomas was in a good mood when we arrived back at the office. A telegram and a wire transfer had arrived ahead of us.

The Baron had not only paid our usual fee in full he had added a twenty percent bonus for what he described as service above and beyond.

He wrote he was grateful for the recovery of the journal and his children.

It was hard for me to think of Bolt and Stitch as children given their appearance.

A month after our adventure in Limberburger I received a large envelope with a Limberburger postmark. It was addressed to me personally.

I placed the envelope flat on my cluttered desk. The sound of cars and trucks outside the office window filled the vacant air. I frowned and eased back in my chair my eyes fixed on the envelope. The spring on the pedestal beneath my chair squeaked softly.

Why would they write to me?

I thought about throwing the envelope into the trashcan next to my desk. I ran one hand in smoothing action and realized inside was a photograph.

Curiosity kills the detective.

I sighed and picked the envelope from the desk and tore off one end. The photograph inside was a family portrait of the Frankenstein's. Scrawled across the photograph were the words:

Thanks for everything

Love, stitch

In the photograph were the Baron and the Baroness looking as I had met them. But Bolt and Stitch appeared to be around eighteen years old. As I'd suspected the children of the monster had been creating new bodies for themselves at the cheese factory and, when they were fully formed, the Baron transferred their old brains into the new bodies.

The Baron must have been unable to find suitable young subjects when he <u>created</u> his children. Now it appeared that situation had been rectified. Monsters create monsters.

How many of them roam the earth? Who would ever believe me that Frankenstein's children are making monsters?

Madness. Utter madness.

Dear, reader I'm going to close this case as a crime of teenage rebellion. Monstrous and ancient the Frankenstein kids may be like teenagers everywhere who sometimes sow a few wild oats. But in their case they sow a few wild monsters.

Only The Worthy

Sydney Gideon wasn't going to be happy his foreman had ignored his orders not to open the thousand-year-old stone sarcophagus. Sure, the man wanted to remove the White-Hilt from its long hidden resting place by himself. But from what Nick had heard Gideon didn't trust anyone. Even his own foot solders. This disaster would only serve to reinforce the leader of the Brother's paranoid delusions.

Why are billionaire's always such nut jobs?

Nick Sparta engaged the filter on his auto-focus binoculars just as the sphere of brilliant golden flame began to consume the excavation site. He watched the white-hot fire render the flesh from the bones of the excavation crew as it swept over them. The massive excavator melted into slag, as did other smaller work vehicles scattered around the site. A growling, fierce wall of death enveloped men and equipment so fast there was no chance for them to escape, or even time to scream. The flames were like a ravenous beast in search of fresh prey. Everyone within half a mile of the sword was now charred into dust, but at least their deaths had been swift.

"Small mercies," Nick murmured under his breath.

He scanned the devastation with the binoculars looking for any signs of life and found none.

No doubt in the last millisecond of his life the foreman must have realized he should have waited for the Priests of the Brotherhood. The foreman would have no second chance to misjudge matters. "Greed so often courts disaster," Nick sighed.

Nick hoped his own life wouldn't end that way — in a flaming nightmare resulting from his own stupidity.

From his camouflaged listening post, hidden amongst boulders the size of bungalows, over a mile from ground zero, Nick shrugged.

Poor bastards, he thought. But better them than me.

When you're in the world-domination business you have to expect collateral damage. Gideon certainly did.

The white-hot flame dissipated into the cold air. This was accompanied by the crackle of static discharge. It didn't take long for the damp Queen Charlotte Island winds to return to send a chill through his all weather gear after the wave of superheated air had passed over him.

He consoled himself with the thought that the icy rain had finally given way to a constant drizzle. For the past three weeks he'd been camped out on this wind-and-rain swept island to observe the Brotherhoods retrieval operation. Not even hot coffee warmed his insides anymore.

Just as he was about to give up hope of finding anyone alive he spotted someone at the edge of his field of vision. He lay face down on the beach. His head-to-foot black clothing contrasted against the grey sand beach. Anywhere else in the world the smooth sandy beach would be an ideal tourist spot. As the weather in the Haida Gwaii archipelago was not conducive to sun worshipers it meant there was a good chance the survivor wasn't a tourist.

In the dim light Nick thumbed the button to remove the filter. The contrast sharpened and he engaged the zoom feature to focus on the unmoving body. If the man was alive he was the lone survivor of the wrath of the Dyrnwyn.

According to Welsh legend the magical sword had once belonged to Rhydderch Hael, one of the Three Generous Men of Britain. The old tales said that when an unworthy man drew the Dyrnwyn, or White Hilt, from its scabbard he would burn. If drawn by a worthy man the fire from the White Hilt would aid him in his rightful cause. Given today's events, it would seem the legend contained more truth than most. Problem was what cause would an ancient magical sword consider worthy?

The good news for the Brotherhood was that this part of the Charlottes was about as remote an area on Earth as it got. This meant the destruction of the local ecosystem would go unnoticed — at least for a while. Nick doubted if any of the government owned spy satellites were tasked to scrutinize this heap of volcanic rock in the North Pacific. There were no tactical assets of interest to the world powers in these islands. Except now, with the release of this much electro-magnetic discharge, he expected the level of interest by the world powers was about to rise. And quickly. Time was short. He needed to make a sat-call.

He set the binoculars down and peered into the mist. The twitching survivor was about two thousand yards from his position. A frown creased Nick's tanned forehead.

The Brotherhood's support vessel, with its helicopter, still rode the waves offshore. Since the chopper hadn't lifted off yet he might have time. If he could get to the survivor before the rescuers came, he might have the lead he needed to find out where the Brotherhood planned to take the sword, and what they planned to do with it.

Given past history both he and his employer suspected the Brotherhood's worldwide search for the Thirteen Treasures of Britain was the precursor to a much larger scheme. His mission was to find out what they were planning and, if need be, find a way to stop them. If he failed his employer would be forced to play the nuclear card. It could mean a lot of collateral damage.

He made his decision.

He shoved the binoculars into the holster on his belt. He then slipped out from behind the camouflage screen and began to pick his way across the rocks. His boots and gloves were designed to grip ice so he was able to move as fast as the local wildlife across the slick seaweed-coated rocks.

Nick kept his profile as low as possible as he moved toward the beach. His brown eyes flitted in the direction of the support vessel. Though visible through the mist, he thought he saw the rotor blades on the helicopter begin to turn. He felt his abs tighten.

If the Brotherhood discovered him here he was dead. Section N had lost three agents in the past three years attempting to get close to the Brotherhood's operations. He was the only one who'd managed to get this far. In fact, he was the only one still alive. And he wanted to stay alive at least as much as he wanted to track the bastards down.

If he messed up the mission would be compromised. His gut told him failure was not an option. The clock was ticking, and Nick had been at this game far too long not to listen to his gut.

Time to move faster.

He stepped onto the sand just as the sky began to brighten. He could see the black clouds were clearing in the east. He estimated it would be dawn in less than half an hour. While his stealth suit was good, he knew he could be seen against the contrast of the sand, in the light of day.

He figured his chances of succeeding before the helicopter arrived were at nine point two-seven percent.

He would barely have time to retrieve the survivor, if he was in any shape to talk, and get back under cover, before retreating to his listening post. The sword would have to wait.

He glanced at the support ship and saw the black shape of the helicopter lift into the air.

He ran for the target.

Nick estimated there was a thousand yards between him and the survivor. He closed the distance fast.

Nick dropped to his knees in the wet sand beside the still form. Still breathing —good. Nick grabbed the guy's thin arms and heaved the body over his shoulders.

The guy's lighter than I expected.

Nick ran for cover. His breath came in gasps.

He stole a quick glance in the direction of the inbound helicopter. He saw it was headed for the still smoking excavation site, not for the beach. His odds of not being spotted had just improved.

Nick finally reached the cover of the boulders. He moved to a spot out of line of sight with the beach. He slipped the limp body off his shoulders and placed him on the ground, the guy's back against a massive boulder.

The man's head slumped to his chest and his arms hung loose at his sides. He was dressed in a chocolate brown winter parka with brown fur around the hood, hiking boots, waterproof pants, and thick winter gloves. A navy blue balaclava hid his face.

For all Nick knew, it could be Santa Claus in there under all those clothes

Nick sat down on his haunches next to his charge and hung his head. He took several depth breaths, letting his heart rate return to normal.

He rose to his feet to peek around the boulder. The helicopter had landed a few yards shy of the destroyed excavation site. It didn't look like they'd seen him. Just to be on the safe side he had to get back to his camouflaged listening post.

He turned back to study the survivor. He was slim, probably weighted no more than a hundred and twenty-five pounds, medium height, about five nine or so, with smallish hands.

The survivor was a woman.

"This could be interesting," Nick said.

He removed the balaclava from her head. As he did shoulder length, hair the color of copper wire, spilled onto her narrow shoulders. She wasn't a model beauty, but certainly pretty. Her skin was pale. Her rosy cheeks bore the orange freckles common of true redheads. She was breathing.

Score one for the good guys.

He reached for the canteen he kept attached to the tool belt around his waist. After the cap was removed he raised her head and, after taking a sip to moisten his own dry mouth, splashed cold water on her face. She moaned softly and her eyes opened to slits. "Uhhh," she murmured. She threw her head back and it struck the rock. "Owww."

Her left hand went to the spot where her head had contacted the stone. "Where am I?" she said as she rubbed the back of her head.

"Same place you were before. The Charlottes," said Nick. He imagined after the explosion and striking the rock she must have the worst headache since Moses brought the plagues to the Pharaoh. He smirked.

The woman glared at him. "What's so funny?"

136

"Nothing. Just a little dark humor is all." Nick shrugged. "Sorry, it's a weakness in my line of work."

She nodded. "Owww. It's not funny."

"Yeah. I agree. Can you stand?"

"Yes, I think so." He held her hand then gripped her arm in his other hand to help steady her. She stood slowly; using the smooth boulder rock as a backstop.

"I'm sorry about this, but we have to get off the beach and back to my listening post." He nodded toward the group of four men who had disembarked from the helicopter. They were headed for the stone sarcophagus at the epicenter of the blackened sand and earth.

The woman squinted at the scene and her rosy cheeks paled. "We have to stop them," she said then teetered. One hand went to her forehead. Her eyes closed. She almost fell until Nick wrapped one muscular arm around her narrow waist. He then carried her limp body across the rocky landscape.

***

Once behind the stealth shield Nick set his new charge on his single padded camp chair. He sat across from her on a rock.

He removed the form-fitted hood of his stealth suit and gasped for breath. The suit was effective for surveillance operations, but it was too warm for running cross-country with a hundred pound weight slung over your shoulder. The designers should add an air conditioner feature.

He blew air from his lungs and then took in several more deep breaths.

After a few moments the woman opened her eyes. "So that's what you look like," she said with a twinkle in her voice. "Not bad."

Nick smiled. "What did you mean when you said we had to stop them? Who is them?"

"Sydney Gideon." Nick looked at her quizzically. "My employer," she continued. "The one after the sword."

Nick shrugged as if he didn't know what she was talking about. She erupted in a mirthless laugh. "The one who nearly killed us." Her expression became sly. "Com'on, Mr...?"

"Nick Sparta."

"Well, Mr. Sparta —"

"Call me Nick."

She nodded. "OK, Nick. My name's Dr. Tiffany Wilson-Tyne by the way — you must be the best equipped tourist in history."

Nick offered a tight-lipped smile. "Oh, just a few comforts from home. You know what they say, never leave home without them."

She looked at the surveillance equipment Section N had provided him.

It included; a directional microphone with a two mile range, a telescopic camera with enough memory for five thousand photographs, an all weather satellite laptop computer powerful enough for use in the Mars Lander, and a satellite phone that allowed him to connect with anywhere on the planet.

Her green eyes lingered on the satellite phone. "Who are you? Really."

Nick smirked. He needed time to think. How did he know he could trust this woman? What was her connection to the White Hilt, and the Brotherhood? Was Sydney Gideon just her employer or was he her Svengali?

"Doctor, huh? Gynecology? Obstetrics?"

She chuckled. "Archaeology actually. Now who are you?" Her tone suggested persistence.

Nick opened the Velcro pouch on his belt and pulled out the faux CIA identification card he carried. He handed it to her.

She looked at it. As she did her lips became a thin line and her brow wrinkled. "CIA? What are you doing here?"

"I should be asking you why an archaeologist is helping the Brotherhood. Whose grave have you robbed? That explosion was rather nasty."

Tiffany sighed and her shoulders slumped. "I know. The idiot foreman shouldn't have touched the sword. I warned him not to touch it, but he ignored me, obviously." She shook her head. "Max wasn't very bright. Though, to be honest, I had no idea the legend of the Dyrnwyn's power was true. After all I'm a scientist not a soothsayer." Her voice carried a hint of regret.

"How did you happen to be on the beach?"

"We were ordered to wait for the priests, so I went for a walk."

Nick doubted she would have left the site of a major archaeological find for the sake of a little exercise.

When the University of British Columbia team announced they'd found an ancient shipwreck on a remote island in the Queen Charlotte chain it had started a firestorm of controversy. Particularly amongst the local aboriginal population, who claimed the vessels remains were of native origin and their property. When it was determined the wreck was a Welsh vessel from pre-history, the academic and scientific community silenced the native protests.

Stone tablets, found in the nearby settlement, told of the exile of a great Welsh King named Owain Dangwyn. Old Welsh legends said he was the last owner of the White Hilt. And the last King to wield the swords power. The sarcophagus had to be his final resting; the place where the long lost White Hilt was buried.

When the Brotherhood discovered the location of the magic Welsh sword, one of the Thirteen Treasures of ancient Britain, Gideon dispatched his team to retrieve it.

Section N had been monitoring the Brotherhood's ships, planes, and other assets, for months. When their ship sailed, its abrupt departure set off alarm bells.

The satellite net computer model projected the vessel was headed for the northern Canada pacific coast. Satellite surveillance showed the speed the ship traveled meant the vessels turbines were on maximum power for a period longer than they were designed for.

They were in one hell of a hurry and Section N needed to find out why. It was as if someone had poked a wasp's nest with a stick.

Within ten hours Nick was dropped by high altitude Halo parachute jump, to lessen the chance of detection. Within a day of his arrival an unmanned drone submarine delivered the supplies he needed. Once the mission was complete he'd leave the island using the submarine.

The plan was he'd secure the White Hilt, but so far all he'd done was surveillance. That was until today.

The situation had become more complex.

His job was now to risk manage the changing parameters until his mission objectives were achieved.

The arrival of the woman, which the data models suggested was an acceptable risk, due to her knowledge of Brotherhood operations, was still a wild card in his computations.

"What does the Brotherhood intend to do with the sword and the Thirteen Treasures?"

Tiffany's green eyes narrowed and a look of annoyance flashed through her emerald eyes. She crossed her arms. "Sorry but I signed a confidentiality agreement. I can't discuss it."

Nick stood and stepped toward her. His expression became hard. "Listen, I don't know you very well, but this man Gideon you work for is a very dangerous man. Once your job is done he will kill you."

He was surprised when a smirk replaced her doubtful expression. "Nick, I think that's where you're mistaken. I'm in this for the money. Nothing more. "

Four men, with automatic weapons at the ready, burst through the stealth shield.

Nick knew then he'd been played.

***

The ropes held his arms behind his back. No matter how he struggled he'd been unable to budge the knots so much as a fraction of a millimeter.

At this rate I'll be free in fifty years. I'll be terminated with extreme prejudice long before then.

After being on land for so long the movement of the ship felt good. The commando-in-charge of the assault had backhanded him during the capture. Nick could still taste the blood in his mouth from the cut in the soft flesh inside his mouth.

He computed the odds of his survival. He estimated his chances were less than five percent. There really was only one option left to him, but it would take the opportune moment to ensure success.

As he was shoved up the ships ladder he caught a glimpse of the helicopter, as it lowered the sarcophagus to the landing pad. He was slammed face first into the freshly painted cold steel wall of the corridor.

Spots clouded his vision as the hulking man grabbed him by his collar and guided him along the narrow corridor.

Nick's boots failed to make contact with the deck.

The guard grunted and poked him hard in the kidneys with the barrel of his weapon. Nick winced in pain and stepped into a room.

The room contained a long gray table along one wall, and two armless wooden chairs. Otherwise it was empty. There wasn't even a porthole.

The guard pushed him toward one of the chairs. The guard used one meaty hand to press him into the chair. He then pulled out a long bladed knife from a holster on his hip.

For a moment, Nick thought the guard was going to kill him. The guard cut the rope from his wrists. It seemed the Brotherhood had other plans for him.

This would be his only chance to escape. The guard stepped back and trained his machine pistol on Nick. "Don't try anything or…" Nick nodded. He understood threats.

After the guard lowered his gun he looped the strap over his left shoulder. He made the mistake of losing eye contact as he moved around the chair. His right hand held a plastic wrist restraint, while his left was wrapped around the machine gun's strap. Nick knew that if the man succeeded in tying him to the chair he was history.

It was time to act.

As the guard moved parallel to Nick's left side, Nick leapt to his feet and head butted him. Stunned by the blow, and already off balance, the guard stumbled away and fell.

He slammed hard face-first into the wall. There was a bone-crushing smack. The impact must've broken the guard's nose because blood squirted over the wall.

Nick moved with inhuman speed to grip the guard's bull-like head in his hands. With a violent jerk of the guards head Nick snapped his neck. _Crack_.

The guard went limp. He sagged to the floor to land in a heap.

Nick froze as someone behind him applauded.

He turned and saw a robed figure behind him flanked by two more of the burly guards.

"Well done, Mr. Sparta."

"Who's next?" Nick said.

A wicked smile spread over the robed man's chiseled features. He placed his fists on his hips. This parted the priestly robe to reveal the holstered pistol on his right hip, and the hilt of a sword in a scabbard on his left. The two guards raised their machine guns to point them at Nick. "I'm afraid you may well be next, Agent Sparta."

***

The robed priest stood beside the stone sarcophagus. Nick stood near the ships rail flanked by two guards. Seven other armed guards encircled the group.

By now the sun had come out. The warmth of the sunlight felt good on Nick's face after the weeks of rain. The sea air seemed fresher somehow. Seagulls swooped overhead, their cries carried in the gentle breeze that had sprung up. The ship rolled over the ocean swells to dance on its anchor.

Dr. Tiffany stood beside the Priest, her green eyes filled with excitement. She looked like a kid on Christmas morning. Not that Nick had ever experienced Christmas morning.

A crane lifted the stone lid of the sarcophagus into the air and lowered it the deck. Thump.

The Priest of the Brotherhood explained he planned to keep Nick alive for now. Nick would report the successful recovery of the White Hilt by the Brotherhood.

Nick made all the clichéd statements about how mad their plan was, and that Section N wasn't about to standby and let them take over the world, etcetera, but the priest was undeterred.

In fact, he seemed to relish the idea of the nuclear option. He described it as the cleansing. A chance for the world to begin again.

These people are nuts.

"Doctor, I want you to be the first to hold the sacred sword of Rhydderch Hael. Please take it out of the grave."

Tiffany's eyes went wide. "Uhhh…I'm not sure I should. I mean after what happened to Max and the others…" Her lean frame began to tremble even though she still wore the heavy winter parka.

The expressionless eyes of the Priest gazed at her. "Nonsense, Doctor. I want you to have the honor."

Nick realized the priest wanted her to go first. While Nick didn't wish her ill will, he doubted Tiffany Wilson-Tyne was worthy of the swords magic. After all, she was in it for the money.

Nick computed the odds and determined his initial assessment was the only way to stop them now. The survival of the human race was all that mattered.

It was time to act.

Nick grabbed the guard on his left by his wrist. His momentum had caught the man off balance. Nick used the man's weight against him to slide him into another guard.

They fell in a heap of twisting arms and legs. Unable to react in time the other seven guards began to frantically un-sling their weapons.

Before they could level the guns at him, Nick reached into the sarcophagus and had the White Hilt out before anyone could stop him.

Silence. Men frozen with fear. The sound of the breeze and the seagulls, unfazed by the humans' battles.

144

"No one shoots," the priest warned the guards. They looked at each other in confusion, then lowered their weapons.

"Agent Sparta, you may well be worthy to hold the White Hilt, but only I know how to control its power," the priest said.

He held out his left hand offering to take the ancient sword, while his right moved across his body to grasp the hilt of his own sword. All the priest had to do was shoot Nick and take the sword. But there was no way he could.

Nick knew members of the Brotherhood prided themselves on being experts in the ways of ancient combat. Since Nick had a sword the priest could only use a sword to kill him.

Nick raised the White Hilt until the sharp tip of the gleaming blade was pointed skyward. "It is written that only the worthy may use the Dyrnwyn, provided his cause is just," he said.

"He's right," breathed Tiffany. Her eyes were wide with fear.

She edged back as if she hoped to escape if the flames were to engulf them.

"I must have the sword. It is the destiny of the Brotherhood to possess its power," said the priest.

He drew his sword and charged at Nick. His swarthy features were twisted by rage and determination.

The priest was about to bring his sword's blade down to slice his shoulder when Nick stepped aside and brought the blade of the Dyrnwyn down to strike the priest's skull.

The blade sliced through flesh and bone. The priest emitted a snarl of rage and pain as blood spurted from the mortal wound. But he wasn't done. The priest turned and swung his blade to slice open Nick's right arm from the elbow to the wrist. Blood flowed to the deck.

Flames engulfed the priest's head. The dying man managed to emit a single tortured scream as the flame spread to engulf his body.

He collapsed to the deck in a heap of flaming skin and bone.

Nick turned off the pain receptors beneath his artificial skin. He ran for the ships rail. The guards, too stunned by the horror of the priest's death to stop him, watched as Nick vaulted over the ships railing and disappeared.

He landed in the ocean with a splash.

Satellite maps of the seabed showed the support ship was anchored on the edge of an underwater shelf. The shelf on the starboard side of the ship fell away to the deepest trench in the North Pacific. Nick would be buried in the soft silt of the seabed with the sword.

Nick sank until the sunlight was unable to penetrate.

The weight of the sword was sufficient to send him deep into the abyss. He would reach the muddy seabed within a few minutes.

He deactivated his internal locator beacon. He had stopped anyone from possessing the power of the sword. He knew even someone with the best of intentions would be tempted to misuse the power of the Dyrnwyn. For the betterment of mankind the sword must be lost forever.

As Nick sank into the inky blackness he shut down his synaptic pathways. His internal program manager shifted into hibernation mode.

Just before he lost consciousness his artificial intelligence system entered the final stage for safe mode, he felt satisfaction. His mission objectives had been achieved, not exactly as his programmers had planned. Nick Sparta might not continue but the human race would survive, at least for now. In Section N failure was never an option. Just as it was foretold in the ancient scriptures the White Hilt would once again be in the hands of only the worthy.

Big Hairy Deal

FOR ONCE I WASN'T IN THE OFFICE when our future four-legged client bounded passed me snarling at screaming civilians. At the time I was concentrating on squeezing a grapefruit at Mo's Fruitland on Bleeker street, near the office.

My office is located on the third floor of a three-story, mold-covered brick walk-up above Bleeker Street in the city of Vancouver. And not the pretty-multi-cultural-Mecca-Vancouver by the sea you're thinking of--the one on the west coast of Canada. My Vancouver is the one sucked into the dark, gloomy alternate reality where paranormal is normal.

Today is a day like most days. I'm squeezing fruit watching a crazed vendor swinging a broom in self-defense at a werewolf and I know I have to do something about it. It's my job.

With my partner we own and operate a private detective agency. We solve problems in the neighborhood. Unusual problems. No, not plumbing or electrical problems, those are someone else's problem. We deal with the who-ya-gonna-call kinda problems.

In an alternate universe I used to be an agent for the Legal Investigative Protection Service. Yes, I am the original Woman From L.I.P.S.

Impressive I know, but when Matt and I were accidentally sucked into a space-time portal we ended up here where the L.I.P.s doesn't exist. A girl with my skills has to have something to do so naturally we became PI's.

Matt Butcher, former zombie, and my some time boyfriend, is my partner in our little two-person agency, Abby-Normal Investigations.

Our motto is: We take on any case no matter how weird, how supernatural, how small, how big, or how much you want to pay. Justice is our middle name.

My middle name is actually Mabel, but I hate it.

I introduce myself using only my first and last name. "Armstrong, Aloha Armstrong. Private Dick" has a nice ring to it. Aloha Mabel Armstrong? Yuk.

As far as I'm concerned my middle name is as big a secret as the combination on the suitcase with the nuclear launch codes.

Anyway, Matt and I handle the cases the cops are too scared to, or the ones they have no idea how to. Zombies, vampires, midgets (some of my best friends are midgets), swamp monsters, and all sorts of alien life forms are our traditional client base. Let me tell you aliens are the worst tippers. Anyone got change for a Zelbot drudge?

Yeah sure, every once in a while a real person walks through the door, but they're usually looking for the can.

So today, as I'm squeezing the grapefruit, this werewolf suddenly appears and starts tearing up the fruit stand and threatening to eat the customers. Since I'm a lot like Batman (other than the shoulder-length-copper-red wavy hair, knee-high-spike-heeled leather boots, leather mini-skirt, and mid-rift-barring-too-tight tee we are exactly the same), in that I carry every sort of utility item in my purse. Naturally, I come to the rescue.

I pull a werewolf biscuit from my purse and quickly have this werewolf understanding who's the alpha. In fact, soon the beast on its back whimpering like a puppy and I'm scratching its belly.

It doesn't take long before there is the inevitable shape shift and a naked woman lay at my feet and I'm scratching her belly. Ok, I know this sounds weird (and it is), but in this universe weird is my business.

I stand. "You okay?"

She blinks, with her arms and legs still in air in that aren't-I-the-cute-little-puppy position, then said, "Yeah, I think so." A frown creased her brow. "But I'm not sure."

I sense there is more to this woman's story, I just need to dig a little deeper. I need Matt.

***

Once back at the office I make her cup of green tea for our prospective client while Matt gives her blanket to cover herself. She's shivering by now, not a surprise given it rains most of the year. I glance out the window overlooking Bleeker street in time see a flash of lightning brighten the gray overcast sky. Really? Does it have to be gloomy all the time?

Our office is located downtown, in the seedier section of the city, in a building way past its prime. Not that it's going to be here much longer.

Foreign developers bought blocks of the seedier parts of downtown a few years back, and have built several towers worth of condos in the midst of the cesspool. For eight hundred grand you get a closet with a great view of another closet with a great view. Did I buy one of these expensive shoeboxes? Yeah, right, I may work with the undead but I'm not brain dead.

Anyway, the woman, her name is Lizzie Harris, turns out to be an accountant for a mad scientist bent on world domination.

Why anyone would want to dominate this world is beyond me. The place is such a mess, and you'd have to spend all your time running around fixing stuff. Like I'm the handy-woman type? I don't think so.

Matt, with his calm demeanor, is, as usual, able to elicit information Lizzie doesn't realize she even knows. Square jawed Matt, with his wavy brown hair, intense hazel eyes, and aura of confident strength makes most women weak at the knees. He's beautiful and he's mine. A least for now.

In the dark days before Zombie Away, Matt suffered from zombieitis. I often wonder if his inner calm comes from his days as a zombie. He seemed so care free when we first met. Maybe if you know you're going to turn to dust soon you have a different outlook on life. I'm no shrink so what do I know?

Our on-again, off-again relationship suffers because he has no sense of humor. He's so darned serious all the time and it drives me nuts. He says I'm too sarcastic to be a good detective. It's our sore point.

Lizzie tells us the mad scientist has been cooking the books and stealing from his investors. Who knew mad scientists had investors?

I sit half listening to her explanation of his embezzlement scheme, thinking about my hair appointment this afternoon, not particularly caring about any of this, (you invest in the evil scheme of a crazed genius what do you expect?) until she says he also applied for some government research grants under false pretenses.

"I think you just threw us a bone," I blurted silencing Matt and Lizzie.

Lizzie looked at me slack-jawed and the corners of Matt's mouth curled slightly then dropped back into the familiar grim line. He'd never admit it but I just made him laugh.

"Is that a crack?" Lizzie said indignantly.

Oops. Time for damage control. "Huh, sorry, no not at all." I tried my best let's-be-pals smile but she glared at me. Her angular features were pinched like she'd sucked on a lemon. Werewolves can be touchy about their inner wild child.

"What I'm referring to is the part about your boss ripping off the government. I don't like that." I lowered my voice. "I mean, I really don't like that."

Lizzie shriveled deeper into the worn wing chair and gripped her teacup tighter causing the color to drain from her knuckles. I swear I saw fear in her eyes. A frightened werewolf is just pitiful.

I may have gone too intense, but then sometimes you have to let the client know you're not all sweetness and light. It's especially important, when you're a hot looking babe like me, that people see your serious side.

Matt gazed at me and gave me the slight nod he does when he's telling me to cool it. He rolled his shoulders beneath his perfectly tailored double-breasted suit, then shifted his gaze to Lizzie. "Sorry about her. She gets a little carried away." Her paused to clear his throat. "What she means is the government will pay us to find out more about your boss' embezzlement scheme."

Lizzie grinned at him like a schoolgirl on her first date. I suppressed the urge to gag, and crossed my arms over my bosom, determined to keep quiet.

Matt continued. "What's your boss' name."

"He's quite mad you know?" Matt nodded. "His name's Tres Zero."

***

The Zero's had been haunting us since we started this agency.

In fact even before that when we stopped the father, Arnold Zero, from stealing the formula for Zombie Away. Then we stopped his son, Uno when he threatened to turn the whole world into zombies.

A Google search confirmed Tres Zero is the illegitimate son of Uno Zero and the bearded lady from the Dingaling Brothers Circus.

Yup, we're up to our necks in zero's, again.

This simple case of embezzlement had suddenly turned into a race against time to stop another Zero from taking over the world.

My heart pounded in my ears and my blood coursed through my veins. It's s days like this when ya know this crime fighting gig just never gets old.

***

We arrived at Castle Zero, situated at the end of a windy, dirt road atop Mount Seymour overlooking the city, just as dusk fell. When you live in a place where weather is an issue let me tell you dusk falls hard. The night was as black as the inside of a cookie jar. Not that I know what the inside of cookie jar looks like, but a girl can dream, even when she's always on a diet.

Matt's driving. The '74 Pinto rattled and wheezed its way up the winding road up the side of the mountain. Pelting rain bounced off the roof of our rusting hulk of a car. We stopped outside the ten-foot tall front gates guarding the long gravel driveway. The Pinto sighed as if were relieved to get this far.

No kidding, me too.

It often occurred to me our car might be haunted, which wouldn't be surprising, but that investigation would have to wait for another day. We had tax fraud and a take-over-the-world case going at the same time so our plate was full, thank you very much.

No room for the small stuff.

Lizzie told us she'd pay mucho dollars to get the goods on her boss. And when we had the evidence of fraud we'd turn it over to the government. They pay handsome rewards for stuff like that.

I'm hoping it's enough so Matt and I can take the big vacation we always talked about — or rather, I talk about. He just listens and nods.

And then there's the whole saving the world thing. That's just icing on the cake. I mean we're talking about a mad scientist, not a rocket scientist, how serious could it be?

The Pinto's four cylinders chugged, and the fan belt whined and squeaked, as I stared through the streaky windshield at the gates. Along the tops of the steel bars were images of hissing gargoyles and grinning fairy's with mouths full of sharp teeth. Not the most inviting thing I'd ever seen, but not the worst either.

There were those smiling clowns of Slashing, Montana. I shivered. That's an image I'd rather forget, but never could.

"There's an intercom," Matt said, with a nod of his head at the stonewall next to the gates. I squinted into the darkness. Sure enough through the shimmering rain I saw a square black pad with an oval shaped lemon-yellow button affixed to the wall about knee height from the ground.

"Oh, you've got to be kidding." This Zero is a chip of the old woodpile. The button being where it is means he's a little person. It seems in the Zero family all the fruit hangs close to the ground. "Not too far to fall, I guess," I muttered.

"What?" said Matt.

"Nothing. It's a joke."

He nodded, his face hard as steel. "You gonna get us in?"

I flipped a coin on the drive here to determine who would get out if there was a gate. I lost.

I looked down at my expensive leather boots, then at the muddy road, then at Matt. I think he knew there'd be a gate.

I swung the car door open, then pulled my plastic raincoat over my head, and ran to the wall. Mud squished under foot and the smells of the surrounding fir and pine trees filled my senses.

Before I pressed the intercom button I noticed there was what looked like a coin slot on the panel, I hadn't noticed from the car. Odd. Never seen a coin slot on an intercom before. I shrugged and pressed the button.

I waited while rainwater dripped off my coat all around me, and shuffled my feet so my precious leather boots wouldn't sink any deeper into the sucking mud. After what seemed like forever, a gravel crunching voice came over the intercom.

"Yeah?"

I'd practiced my pitch all the way here. I knew Matt grew tired of listening when he started saying every one was pitch perfect, even though some were just stupid and off key.

"Hi, we're from Publishers Habitat Sweepstakes. We have a check for Dear Occupant." I took my finger off the button.

Girl, when your wit is on it's really on.

There was a slight pause then the voice said, "Mr. Occupant doesn't wish to be disturbed. Go away."

I pressed the button again and laughed, "No, wait. Please. That was just a little sweepstakes humor we use round the office. Actually, I have a big fat check for a Mr. Tres Zero. Would Mr. Zero be at home?" Again, I released the button.

I could feel it in my bones, this was gonna work for sure.

There was another pause, only longer this time, then the voice said, "Put fifty cents in the slot and come up to the house. Greta will meet you." The tinny speaker crackled then fell silent.

Yeah, baby you are sooo smooth.

It was then I realized I didn't have any coins on me, and for sure not in my I'm-so-cool-I'm-tiny-purse back in the car. I glanced at the slot. It didn't look like it took bills. I looked to the car with its fading headlights and sagging suspension.

I hoped Matt had exact change.

***

We came back in two hours. Thankfully, the gas station we passed at the bottom of the mountain was still open. The snag-toothed attendant even pumped gas for us so we could get the right change we needed. Ever try to pump exactly two dollars and fifty cents worth of gas? It 'aint easy.

After we got back I first buzzed the house to let them know we had returned, then slipped the coins into the slot.

I ran to the driver's side of the Pinto and climbed in as the tall gates slowly opened on squealing hinges.

Once past the gates the Pinto groaned and popped as it crunched over the gravel driveway. I winced as a rock pinged off the undercarriage. The car had to last another year, at least until I made the final payment.

Finally, we stopped on the circular driveway in front of the two-story ink-black mansion. There were stone steps leading to a heavy oak door with a gargoyle knocker. A row of twenty-foot marble columns stood on either side of the steps holding up an overhang off the sloped roof. The mansion reminded of Scarlet O'Hara's in Gone With the Wind crossed with the Addams Family house.

We got out and walked up the steps to the door. I was grateful for the overhang; it kept us out of the rain.

Matt tipped the edge of his fedora to let the excess rain fall off, (I really love when he wears his hat. It makes him look all Sam Spade.) then used the gargoyle knocker to announce us. As the echo of the thump, thump dissipated the door began to swing aside. They must have oiled the hinges recently because it did so soundlessly.

I expected the interior to be a gloomy as the exterior, but was surprised to find a well-kept foyer with a polished wood floor, a maroon-navy Persian rug, and a rose wood side table with a matching chair beside it. On the table was an antique lamp that cast a soft glow over the woman who greeted us.

A gentle smile played across her thin lips. "Hello, Mr. Butcher and Miss Armstrong," she said, gazing at us over her reading glasses in a way reminiscent of a school marm. She was short—no more than four-foot eleven—with grey hair pulled into a tight bun atop her oval-shaped head. Her navy and red paisley dress, that ran past her knees, hung loosely on her small frame and on her tiny feet she wore plain black slip-on shoes.

"I'm the doctors housemaid, Greta."

"Hello, Greta," I said, deciding in the interests of time to use the direct approach I'm best known for. "We're here to see the doc. We hear he's planning on taking over the world."

A puzzled frown formed on Greta's forehead. "I'm sorry, dear but I don't know what you're talking about. Dr. Zero is trying to help people."

Matt interrupted before I could rebut the old lady. "Sorry, Greta, my partner gets a little carried away some times." He glanced at me and raised an eyebrow.

Oh, I get it. Good detective. Bad detective.

I nodded but scowled at him to add to the illusion I was angry. Which I actually was, but since it enhanced my role as the bad dick I decided to play along.

Greta smiled at Matt in that creepy, cougar-like way. I swear Matt could charm the pants off Ann Coulter on her worst day.

He continued. "We've come a long way to see Mr. Zero." He patted the left breast of his suit jacket. "We have the check."

"Yes, of course. I'll take you to his laboratory." She turned and started to walk away. "Right this way."

She led us through the quiet house filled with more antique furniture, Persian rugs, the woods floors polished and gleaming. We passed a grandfather clock that chimed the half hour. The black arms on the brass face told me it was eleven-thirty already.

Finally, she led us into a massive library with floor-to-ceiling shelves filled with hard cover books. I stared at the old lady. Is she kidding? The secret entrance to a mad scientist's laboratory in the library is so old school. It's a cliché.

She walked to another door at the other end of the room then used a brass key; she withdrew from the pocket of her dress, to unlock it. She swung it open and inside was the laboratory complete with a work bench with racks of test tubes, and humming machines for I-don't-know-what, and a man who could only be Dr. Tres Zero.

His lab is on the first floor, not the dusty basement? Sometimes even I can be wrong.

As I suspected, Tres Zero was a little person with slicked oil-black hair, a neatly trimmed goatee and mustache. He wore a gray vest under his white lab coat and white running shoes on his feet. To me he looked more like a miniature version of Sigmund Freud than a mad scientist, but looks can be deceiving.

"Hello," said Zero with a grin, his thumbs hooked off the pockets of his vest. A chain from a pocket watch hung across his belly between the vest pockets. "Can I have the check, please. I have a lot of work to do before midnight."

Midnight! That must be zero hour. (Com'on, you know someone had to say it.)

"What happens at midnight?" said Matt, his hazel eyes casually scanning the laboratory.

"You two and the others will be my slaves," Zero said, like he was ordering a skinny latté with a twist.

My stomach muscles tightened. We were about to take a trip on the crazy train. Good thing Matt's the boy scout of our little agency. He always comes prepared.

Glancing at the old woman I saw her being to shape shift. The old lady gave way to a snarling, flesh-eating werewolf, and I'm fresh out of werewolf biscuits.

Matt reached into his suit jacket and pulled out his .45 automatic. Without warning he turned the gun on the old lady-werewolf and shot her twice. Once in the chest, the other in the middle of her forehead. The first shot stopped her in her tracks, the other blew out the back of her head scattering her brains across the lab. The bullets slammed her backward and she landed hard then shifted back to her human form. It wasn't a pretty sight.

"Silver bullets?" I said.

Matt shrugged. "Of course."

In the commotion Zero ducked under the laboratory bench and disappeared into a trap door in the floor.

Suddenly gas jets lit up with blue and red flames along the parameter of the walls. Like all mad scientists Zero had a self-destruct-when-discovered-obsession so the house and all its contents, including the evidence of fraud, was going up in flames. If we wanted to avoid going up with it we needed to leave right now. There'd be no time to search the house.

We may have stopped Zero's evil plan for world domination, whatever it is, but our payday was gone.

***

The next day we sat in the office with our feet on top of our desks discussing the Zero case, hoping the next client would soon darken our door.

"What do you think Zero was up to?"

Matt shrugged then took a sip from his Mickey Mouse coffee mug. "Werewolves I'd say."

"Werewolves?"

"Yeah, ya know a big hairy deal."

I looked at him and his features were as serious as ever. "You know you just made a joke, right?"

He shook his head. "Nope."

I sighed. "Some day you're gonna slip, and I'm gonna be there to laugh my butt off."

About the Authors

International selling author, Russ Crossley writes romance under the name R.G. Hart, mystery/suspense under the name R.G. Crossley, and science fiction and fantasy under his own. This year there will be re-issues the romantic comedies, Bachelorette: Zombie Edition and Antique Virgin by 53rd Street Publishing, paranormal romantic comedy, Zomopolis, and a new western romance entitled, The Fire In Their Hearts co-authored with R.S. Meger will be published in 2013 by Champagne Books. Also, look for another Aloha adventure, Bloody Betty Queen of the Pirates, coming later in 2013.

In addition the near future suspense novel, The Last Serial Killer by R.G. Crossley was recently released by 53rd Street Publishing in ebook and trade paperback versions early in 2013.

His latest science fiction satire set in the far future, Revenge of the Lushites, is a sequel to Attack of the Lushites released in 2011. The latest title in the series will be released in the fall of 2013. Both titles are available in e-book and trade paperback.

He has sold several short stories that have appeared in anthologies from Pocket Books, St. Martins Press, at Smashwords, Amazon, and other e-retail sites.

With his wife, romance author R.S. Meger, he owns and operates a small press publishing company, 53rd Street Publishing. The company began in April 2011 and now has over one hundred e-book titles and over twenty-five print titles, with more planned in 2013 and 2014.

He is a member of SF Canada and the Greater Vancouver Chapter of Romance Writers of America.

He is also an alumni of the Oregon Coast Professional Fiction Writers Master Class taught by award winning author/editors, Kristine Katherine Rusch and Dean Wesley Smith.

To find a complete listing of his work check out his website http://www.rghart.com, http://russstory.blogspot.com.Razor's blog can be found at http://razorandedge.blogspot.com

Feel free to contact him on Facebook or Twitter. He loves to hear from readers

Other books by the Author

Titles as R.G. Crossley

Short Stories

Razor and Edge Mysteries
The Kidnapping of Billy Buttons
String of Pearls
Death by Clown
Beggin' For Murder
Ragged Ice
The Grand Central Mystery
A Strange Case of Undead Murder

Jazz Stiletto Mysteries
A Day Without Sunshine
Skullduggery

Non-Series Mysteries
Mirror Image
Dangerous Waters
Cape Disappointment
Boomerang
The Watcher of Wayburn Street
The Apprentice
Drip!
A Beautiful Friendship and The Parrot of Doom
Robine's Diary
The Christmas Club
Loose Ends
Splatter Pattern
It Takes Two

Anthologies
The Adventures of Razor and Edge:
Five Tales From The Quirky Detective Team

Novels
A Bad Case of Loyalty
The Last Serial Killer
Shear Murder

Titles as Russ Crossley

Novels
Attack of the Lushites
Revenge of the Lushites

Short Stories
Countdown
Shoeless Moe
Round Up At The Burger Bar:
The Story of Trixie Pug, Parts 1, 2, 3, 4, 5, 6, 7
Five Minutes
Blossom Queen, Barbarian
The Secret
The Family Line
End of the Flies
With Death You Get the Eggroll
The Penguin Sleeps With The Fishes
Only The Worthy
Hero For A Day
End of Empire
Strange Bedfellows
Big Business
A Perfect Crime
The Wise Guy and The Pirates
In Search of the Perfect Cup
T.I.N. Men
The Legend of G and the Dragonettes
The Incredible Mr. Fix-It
Lock Stock and Barrel
Divided Loyalties

Cave of Wonders
A Family Empire
Until We Meet Again
Dragon Rising

Presents Anthology Series
Tales of Urban Fantasy
Five Tales of Bizarre Detectives
Tales of Mystery and Suspense
Tales of Weird Fantasy
Spies, Detectives, & Heroes
Tales of Twisted Crime
Tales of The Unexpected
Tales From Space
10 by Russ Crossley
Round Up At The Burger Bar: The Story of Trixie Pug,
Parts 1- 5 The Beginning
Worlds of Science Fiction and Fantasy
More Tales of Mystery and Suspense
Ladies of the Jolly Roger
Justice Served

Titles as R.G. Hart

Short Stories
Tikka's Big Day
"My Partner the Zombie" —
Hungry For Your Love Anthology
(St. Martin's Press)
Big Hairy Deal
One Red Shoe
A Bad Day in Lunden Texas
Hook Island
Grind Manor
Bloody Betty, Queen of the Pirates

Anthologies
Love Stories

Novels
My Zombie Prince
Antique Virgin
The Fire In Their Hearts
with R.S. Meger (coming soon from Champagne Books)
Zomopolis